Jessica Watkins Presents

CREED

Eyewitness

PHOENIX DANIELS

CREED

by *Phoenix Daniels*

PROLOGUE

Taylor, so engulfed in her thoughts, almost hadn't noticed the dark SUV that was moving dangerously fast behind her. She immediately changed lanes to see if the driver was simply in a hurry. But once the SUV was parallel to her, she was face-to-face with the business end of a firearm. She gripped the clutch and kicked it up to the sixth gear, riding faster than she'd ever ridden, successfully leaving the SUV in the dust. But, all of a sudden, a dark sedan swerved into the same lane, almost clipping her rear tire. When the sedan sped to parallel her right side, Taylor snatched her pistol from the back of her pants. When the barrel of a shotgun extended out of the back window, Taylor fired a succession of shots at the driver. The sedan began to swerve and veer to the side. She must have hit the driver.

Good.

Unfortunately, Taylor's brief celebration was short-lived when she was suddenly, struck from behind and sent flying to the grassy knoll on the side of the expressway. Unable to control the bike, Taylor dropped… *hard.*

She hit the ground screaming, knowing immediately that her shoulder was either broken or badly dislocated. Her vision was blurred by tears, but she knew that she needed to run. Still, no matter how hard she tried, she couldn't move. She could faintly

CREED
by *Phoenix Daniels*

hear cries of agony, and suddenly realized that they were her own. Taylor had never felt such intense pain in her life, and she didn't think it could get any worse, until she was mercilessly flipped onto her back. She howled in agony as her helmet was yanked from her head. Whoever wanted her dead was about to get their wish. Taylor was sure of it. And although she cried, she refused to beg. She took a painful breath and looked directly into the eye of the person that was about to end her life. Her heart nearly stopped when she saw the face hovering above her. To say that she was shocked was a gross understatement. Warm tears escaped her eyes, falling into her ears.

"W-why?" she choked.

Without the mercy of an explanation, he pointed his weapon and fired a shot into Taylor's chest. Her body jerked violently upon impact. As she began to lose consciousness, she realized that a bullet had actually entered her body, and although it burned, it wasn't as painful as she would have assumed. As she looked up at the angry, but familiar face, thoughts of the people she loved danced around in her mind. But just before the world went dark, it was *his* name that she cried out.

CREED
by *Phoenix Daniels*

CHAPTER 1
Four months prior...

TAYLOR

Taylor rolled her eyes during uniform inspection. Because of a ridiculous new rule that officers with tattoos on their arms had to wear long sleeves to cover their ink, inspections were more tedious than ever. She often wondered who down at headquarters had the time to sit and figure out what they could do to fuck with police officers, even more than usual. Working the unforgiving streets of Chicago, one would think that the bosses would try to make life at work a tad bit easier. But no, some fat, white-shirt was actually sitting in his office like, "Ooh, let's fuck with them like this." Nine times out of ten, it was someone who made supervisor because of someone that he knew, someone who'd probably never worked a day on the streets, and surely someone who had never even seen "The Hood."

As she stood for the petty inspection, she tried to remember a time, not long ago, when she was in love with her job.

Taylor was thirty, and she'd been a cop for eight years. She grew up in Roseland, a tough neighborhood on the Southside of Chicago. Her dad was a cop, so being a cop was in her blood.

CREED
by *Phoenix Daniels*

Ever since she could remember, it was always her career path. She didn't mind donning her uniform and strapping on her duty belt to interact with the citizens. She didn't even mind the possible danger that she faced every night. But what she did mind was the politics that came along with the job. If she could work her beat and assist her fellow officers without the drama from the powers that be, her job would be a dream. Maybe then she would even have more time to work on her nonexistent love life.

After roll call, Taylor and the rest of the midnight crew began to file out of the roll call room.

"Montgomery, fall back!" the watch commander shouted over her chattering colleagues.

Taylor rolled her eyes and turned to face her supervisor.

"Yes, sir?"

"You caught a detail. You gotta report back here at eight hundred hours."

Is this motherfucka serious?

"Eight? Sir, when am I supposed to sleep?"

"Reverse seniority," was his dry ass response. "You gotta work a traffic detail for the grand opening of that new mega church."

He stared down at his clipboard. "Umm... Yeah. Worship House."

CREED
by *Phoenix Daniels*

Taylor shook her head, realizing that the police department was the only place of employment where one could be considered a rookie with eight years on the job. She was constantly getting stuck with bullshit details.

"Don't be late!" he ordered as he left the room.

"Yes, sir," Taylor mumbled as she followed him out.

CREED

by *Phoenix Daniels*

CREED

"Governor Creed, your speech for the opening of Worship House," Kenyatta "Kena" Watkins, his executive assistant, offered softly as she placed a few sheets of paper on his desk.

He stared at the paper, seriously wishing that there was a way to get out of making an appearance at yet another megachurch, where the only person that would benefit from its existence was an already rich, politically plugged preacher.

"Kena, is it too much to ask for a natural disaster to get me out of delivering this speech?" Governor Victor Creed half-joked.

Kenyatta smiled and walked out of his office.

Victor snatched the speech off of his desk and skimmed over it.

Blah, blah, blah.

It was yet another mechanical performance that he'd have to put on. He could care less about introducing another megachurch. He was nearing the end of his first term as the governor of Illinois, and he had yet to meet a megachurch with a pastor that actually gave two shits about the community. Maybe there were one or two of them out there, but Victor had yet to meet them. Money, he had learned during his campaign, was the driving

CREED
by *Phoenix Daniels*

force behind most of them. He knew this because during the election, he had bought every last one of their endorsements and paid for every last vote that had ensured his victory. The truth was, the church was most influential in the Black and Hispanic communities, and he needed their support to get elected. So, Victor greased every palm necessary to guarantee his place in the Governor's Mansion.

For Victor, winning the election was not an option. His future in politics had been mapped out long before he was born. Victor Creed Sr. was a retired Illinois State senator and had never allowed any options other than politics for his son's future. Victor was groomed to become president of the United States. He wasn't complaining though. Victor loved being the governor. He loved the power. It was the power that allowed him to do good things for the people of Illinois. Although most people were under the impression that the Republican Party was only interested in making the rich richer, for Victor, that couldn't be further from the truth. He vowed to help those that needed help, and to be fair to those that were well off. He wanted to make the quality of life better for every citizen of Illinois.

Victor tossed the papers onto his cluttered desk and slouched down in his chair. He covered his eyes with his hand and massaged his tense eyebrows. It was only nine o'clock on a

CREED
by *Phoenix Daniels*

Saturday night, and he was already exhausted. But sleep would have to wait, because Kara Edwards wouldn't. Victor had promised his tall, voluptuous, toffee-colored press secretary that he'd have a late dinner with her at her place. It was a promise that he was beginning to regret.

Victor recalled the very first time that she'd walked into his office wearing a skin-tight sweater that showed a suggestive amount of cleavage. He'd wanted a sample, and it was obvious that she had wanted to sample him as well. And although in the beginning she claimed that she wanted the same detached, physical liaison that Victor had wanted, she had become very emotionally attached. He often found himself reminding her that he wasn't interested in a love connection. Likewise, she would reassure him that she was on the same page, but her actions proved otherwise. Kara was becoming possessive and clingy, and Victor realized that they were nearing their end.

Since his wife's untimely death in Louisiana during Hurricane Katrina, Victor just couldn't imagine investing in another relationship. But to all, it seemed that he was the most available bachelor in Illinois, and at thirty-seven, the youngest. Victor was well aware that he was on or near the top of every single woman's wish list.

CREED
by *Phoenix Daniels*

Memories of Rosemary, his late wife, invaded Victor's thoughts. He could see a vivid picture of the beautiful young woman that he had never wanted to marry. It was as though she was standing before him. She had a lustrous mane; the color of wheat and bright blue eyes that were filled with hope and promise. Rosemary was smart and talented; a successful immigration attorney. Victor had loved her, but not enough to marry her. Like a monarchy, Rosemary was handpicked by Victor Sr. She was well-bred from a politically influential family. But like most people of privilege, she was self-centered and spoiled. Rosemary was a mirage; a political hallucination forged by a powerful family. Even her choice of practice, immigration law, was designed to portray a woman of compassion.

The union between Victor and Rosemary had been more of a partnership than that of husband and wife. She was the perfect accessory. But now that she was gone, he had to admit that she was missed.

The shrewd buzz of the intercom snapped Victor back to the present.

"Governor Creed, Kara Edwards is waiting on the line," Kenyatta grumbled, with a noticeable tinge of irritation.

Ever since Kara suggested Kenyatta's termination for not divulging Victor's whereabouts, there was no love lost between

9

CREED
by *Phoenix Daniels*

them. Kara felt that as his press secretary, she had the right to know his every move. But since it was Kenyatta's job to protect his privacy, Victor felt that Kara Edwards had crossed a line and immediately had to force her back into her lane.

"Put her through." Victor snatched the phone off of the cradle after the first ring. "I'm on my way," he said briskly before hanging up. He was not about to give Kara a chance at her usual whining.

Victor stuffed the speech into his briefcase and snatched his suit coat off the back of his chair. As he left his office, he tried to come up with the gentlest way of informing Kara that they were about to share their last night together.

CREED
by *Phoenix Daniels*

CHAPTER 2
TAYLOR

"Gotdamn! It's hotter than Satan's nut sac out here!"

Taylor chuckled at Will's vulgar over-exaggeration. Will was another sucker with no seniority that got assigned to the traffic detail at the megachurch. He was right, however; it *was* hot as hell outside, but Satan's sac was a bit much. It had to be at least ninety degrees out, and most Chicagoans could easily survive ninety-degree temperatures. But factoring in a poly-blend uniform, an unbearably hot baseball cap, and a twenty-pound utility belt digging into her hip, for Taylor, traffic control was the worst kind of torture.

It was ten o'clock. Taylor was only two hours into her day and she was already, ready to go. She hated directing traffic; stopping, waving on, and directing motorists and pedestrians that pretended to be deaf and blind. She'd been cussed out at least four times, and had almost gotten run over twice. Taylor was hot and irritated. She snatched the Velcro on her bulletproof vest, pulled the vest off and tossed it into the back seat of her squad car, knowing that if she got caught without it, she could get written up.

Oh well.

CREED
by *Phoenix Daniels*

As hot as it was, Taylor was willing to deal with a supervisor. She just prayed that no one shot at her. Hell, as tired as she was, they might have been doing her a favor. If she lived, she could rest up in an air-conditioned hospital.

"Heads up, Tay," Will warned with a nudge.

Another caravan of black SUV's were approaching the entrance. Taylor didn't even speculate as to the *important* person that was being escorted into the massive church. She walked over to the sidewalk and held her hand up, stopping vehicles and pedestrians in order to allow the caravan entry into the parking lot. A line of SUV's entered one behind the other, except for the third vehicle in line. When it reached the mouth of the lot, the driver slowed down to a creep. Taylor could see nothing but her reflection in the tinted window, but she couldn't help but feel as if she was being watched. Nonetheless, she continued to hold off the pedestrians until the last vehicle in the caravan passed.

Taylor continued to serve as an armed crossing guard for pedestrians and motorists alike. She held up her white-gloved hand and waved a line of pedestrians, who were on their way to the church, across the street. As if she wasn't already annoyed with the traffic detail, some impatient asshole decided to rest on their horn.

CREED
by *Phoenix Daniels*

"Move!" shouted a woman in a green Honda. "Damn! Get the fuck outta the way," the driver yelled, despite the fact that they were at a church.

Taylor did her best to ignore the rude woman and continued to wave the pedestrians along. But, of course, Taylor's actions only seemed to infuriate the driver even more. She released a series of expletives as she, once again, assaulted everyone with her horn. Taylor snatched her citation book out of her back pocket and walked over to the woman's car. The lady's hostility was evident as she huffed loudly upon Taylor's approach. To no surprise of Taylor, the first words out of the woman's mouth were, "Don't come over here fuck'n with me! I know my rights!"

"Ma'am, did you also know that according to the Municipal Code of Chicago, honking your horn in a non-emergency situation is a citable offense? I need your driver's license and proof of insurance," Taylor said, responding in an unruffled tone.

The driver's mouth dropped open and her eyes became the size of saucers. Apparently, she thought that it was perfectly okay to be disrespectful to Taylor and to impede her from doing her job. But it wasn't okay. Taylor had to summon the patience of Job to keep herself from snatching the ignorant cuss out of her car through the window.

CREED
by *Phoenix Daniels*

Reluctantly, the driver handed over her driver's license, but she tossed her proof of insurance out of the window. Taylor looked down at the insurance card, then back to the woman that was glaring at her with narrowed eyes. As Taylor walked away, leaving the card on the ground, she looked over at Will. He shook his head in disgust and continued to direct traffic. Taylor hopped into her squad car and entered the lady's driver's license number into the portable data terminal. When the results came through, Taylor got a little excited.

She got out and returned to the Honda.

"Ma'am, please put your car in park, step out of the vehicle, and place your hands behind your back."

"This is so fucking stupid! You ain't got shit better to do?!" she shouted in outrage.

"No, ma'am, do you know what's *fucking stupid*? Fucking stupid is honking your fucking horn like a fucking idiot, and cussin' out the police like a fucking idiot, while driving on a suspended license. You have a traffic warrant; *that's* fucking stupid. Now get the fuck out of the car!" Taylor snapped.

Having no other choice, the woman exited her car and put her hands behind her back. Ignoring the crocodile tears and apologies, Taylor led her to the back seat of her squad car.

CREED
by *Phoenix Daniels*

"Watch your head," she warned as she all but shoved the woman into the back seat.

"You got this?" she shouted to Will.

"Yep. See you later," he responded with a wave of his hand.

Knowing full well that she was about to write the hateful woman a plethora of tickets and impound her shit-colored Honda, Taylor couldn't muster up enough guilt for the feeling of delight she felt as she drove the hateful woman into the station.

❋❋❋❋

Hours later, after a grueling day at work, Taylor was relaxing in the new Jacuzzi tub that she had installed in her master bath. She had recently purchased her first home on the South Side. At thirty, she figured it was time. Her new three-bedroom home in Hyde Park was a work in progress. Thankfully, it was a solid brick structure, surrounded by a lovely landscape. Taylor had decided to remodel one room at a time. In the nine months that she'd been there, she'd had the kitchen, the living room, and the master bed and bath remodeled. The guest bedroom and the guest bathroom, along with the basement, would have to wait. She hadn't planned on having any overnight guests anytime soon anyway.

CREED

by *Phoenix Daniels*

"Tay!" she heard her best friend and partner, Maria Mendez, shout from the hallway.

"I'm in the tub!" Taylor shouted back.

The bathroom door swung open, and Maria flew in. She fiddled with the button and zipper of her jeans, before plopping down on the toilet.

"Ahh," she moaned as she relieved herself, with total disregard for Taylor's presence.

"Really, Maria?"

"Whew! Adios mios, mami! I had to pee."

"I'm sorry I gave yo' ass a key."

"The fuck you want me to do? Pee myself?" Maria asked, unrolling a handful of toilet paper.

"Ugh... Wipe ya ass and get out of my bathroom."

Taylor rolled her eyes and turned off the jets, calming the roaring bubbles. Maria had just destroyed the serenity of her bath.

"What did we discuss about boundaries?"

"Heffa, shut up and get out the tub," Maria quipped as she flushed the toilet.

She fastened her pants and washed her hands, drying them on Taylor's drying towel.

"Bitch," Taylor muttered at Maria's back as she left the bathroom.

CREED
by *Phoenix Daniels*

Taylor climbed out of the tub, dried off, and wrapped herself in the towel. When she entered her bedroom, Maria was spread out across her bed, aiming the remote control at the television.

"How was your detail?"

"How do you think it was?" Taylor scoffed. "I'm a disgruntled employee."

Maria chuckled and continued to surf through the channels. Maria was lucky. She had thirteen years on the job and hardly ever got assigned to the same shitty details that Taylor usually got stuck with. Dealing with the ever-changing scheduling needs of the police department was hard enough. But on top of that, Maria had two little girls and a husband at home. Taylor was in awe of the way that Maria managed the day-to-day of her life. Since she was raised in a traditional Mexican household, having a home cooked meal for her family every day was second nature. It didn't matter what time she got home from work, even if it was three in the morning; she would cook an entire meal and store it in the freezer for her family to eat the next day while she was at work.

"Well, it's all over now, and it's our weekend off. Whatcha got planned?"

"Sunday, I'm going fishing at Fox Lake," Taylor responded, with the most enthusiasm she'd had all day.

CREED
by *Phoenix Daniels*

"Eww. Why do you love playing with slimy things every time you get a day off?"

Taylor ignored the look of disgust that Maria gave her and walked over to her dresser. She fished out a pair of pajamas and headed back into the bathroom. She grabbed a bottle of eucalyptus tea scented body lotion from the cabinet and moisturized her skin, before slipping into her pj's.

"You goin' with your papa?" Maria asked, as Taylor reentered the bedroom.

"Yep."

"Your dad's a hillbilly," Maria chortled. "And you know he secretly wishes that you were a boy, don't you?"

"It's not a secret at all," Taylor chuckled.

James and Martha Montgomery, Taylor's mom and dad, were born in Arkansas. They were southerners to the bone. Her dad was raised on a farm. Had it not been for her mom, Taylor believed that her dad would have never left the south. He loved the country life. Hunting, farming, and fishing were her dad's version of a five-star vacation. And, although her mom convinced him to move to Chicago, he managed to continue his hobbies. He joined the police department, but every weekend that he had off, he was on a lake or toting his rifle through a nearby hunting ground, dragging Taylor along every chance he got. But she

CREED
by *Phoenix Daniels*

certainly wasn't complaining. She loved to escape the harsh big city for a small glimpse into a southern existence.

As far as siblings, there was just Taylor and her sister, Nicole. Contrary to Taylor, Nicole wouldn't be caught dead baiting a hook. She was a carbon copy of her uber feminine mother; a lady to the core. She was a buyer for Saks Fifth Avenue and two years older than Taylor. Nicole was also engaged to be married to Jeffrey, an almost too perfect, yuppie, politician. He seemed nice, but almost too nice.

"Damn, girl. Where did you go? I lost you."

Taylor blinked, snapping her thoughts back to Maria, trying to remember the conversation. "I'm sorry. I was just thinking about my sister. Her fiancé had an extra ticket to the State Dinner on Saturday and my overbearing sister is forcing me to go."

"Extra ticket my ass," Maria argued. "That dinner is like a thousand bucks a plate. Ain't no such thing as *extra* tickets."

"That's what the yuppie told her."

"Mmm hmm. So, what are you going to wear?"

"Don't know. Nic said that she was picking out a dress for me."

"Wow. I'm surprised that you're being so cooperative."

"She wore me down," Taylor responded with a shrug. "Anyway, what are you doing this weekend?"

CREED
by *Phoenix Daniels*

"Making dinner and wiping asses. What else?" she said dryly.

"Girl, don't front. That's your version of fun. You love that shit."

"Whatever," Maria mumbled, climbing out of bed. "Speaking of wiping asses, I gotta go."

"Damn, okay. Text me when you get home."

Taylor was a bit confused by Maria's lack of excitement. On a normal day, Maria loved gushing over her family life. She was a bit concerned about her friend, but she didn't want to pry. Nobody's life was perfect every day. She figured that Maria must have been going through a thing and she'd be over it soon.

She followed Maria down the hall, gave her a hug, and locked the front door behind her. She made her way down the hall, back to her bedroom, and then she realized that she still didn't know the reason for Maria's impromptu visit. Maybe she was just in the neighborhood and had to use the washroom. It was a theory that was highly unlikely, but Taylor lacked the amount of rest needed to solve the dilemma. So, she climbed into her bed, deciding to call her friend the next day.

CHAPTER 3

CREED

The governor's mansion was buzzing with activity, but Victor couldn't be more bored. He knew going in that he was going to see much of the same faces of the same people that normally frequented politically fueled social events.

He stood in the corner, watching everyone move about the ballroom and listening to Kenyatta and her assistant brutally pick apart the wardrobe of the other guests. At times, Victor couldn't stop the chuckle that escaped. Kenyatta and Lisa were hilarious; his evening's saving grace.

"Girl, look at Councilwoman Harris in that tight ass dress," Lisa whispered, a bit too loudly. "I need her to invest in some Spanx."

Victor had no idea what spanks were, so he kept quiet.

"Lisa, you know she wasn't raised right," Kenyatta countered. "My soul won't let me pass my threshold without something to suck in all this ass."

Victor laughed out loud, knowing that he shouldn't have. Truth be told, the congresswoman had a nice round ass. It was her nasty disposition that was a deterrence.

CREED
by *Phoenix Daniels*

Victor leaned closer to Kenyatta. "That's enough. Let's go and sit. Maybe they'll start dinner so that we can get the hell out of here."

"Governor Creed, you're a party pooper. Dinner won't be served for another thirty minutes. Besides, you're about to be busy."

Kenyatta jabbed her thumb to the right of Victor; annoyance was evident in her expression. Victor turned to see Kara's approach. She looked beautiful in a navy-blue form-fitting gown. She had her auburn hair in a sculpted updo, and her hazel eyes sparkled with a hint of anger.

"Governor Creed," she greeted tersely, totally ignoring Kenyatta and Lisa.

"Miss Edwards, you're certainly a vision."

If Victor was hoping to ease the tension with a compliment, he realized that he had failed when she responded with, "Apparently, that's of no consequence to you."

"No, it isn't. But you look beautiful nonetheless. Enjoy your evening."

Before she could respond, Victor walked away, gesturing for Lisa and Kenyatta to follow.

"What was that all about?" Kenyatta asked, as soon as they reached Victor's table.

CREED
by *Phoenix Daniels*

"Time for a new starting player," was all Victor said.

"Thank God," Kenyatta huffed. "It's about time, because Kara Edwards got the devil in her. Oh and by the way... you're a whore."

Victor glared at her, never ceasing to be amazed by the things that came out of her mouth.

"That's Governor Whore to you," he rebutted.

"Forget Governor Whore," Lisa chimed. "Look at that fine specimen that just walked in."

Kenyatta turned and Victor followed her line of sight. The ladies were looking at Jeffrey Morgan, the Chicago Water Commissioner. And although Jeffrey's good looks had done nothing for Victor, one of the women that accompanied him was paralyzing. It was the cop that he'd seen the day before. That day she was wearing a uniform that he was sure she hadn't realized was hugging her every curve. Surely, she hadn't noticed the buttons of her shirt holding on for dear life, barely containing her large tits. And she had the most beautiful skin, the color of pecans. Her lips were full and kissable, and her hair was stuffed under her police cap, with a big bushy ponytail hanging down her back. And though he thought she was gorgeous when he observed her directing traffic, her cute tomboy look had nothing on the bombshell walking into the ballroom. Her bushy ponytail had

CREED
by *Phoenix Daniels*

been converted to a wild, curly, lioness' mane, and her curvy body was wrapped in red satin. The color was striking against her bronze skin. The lady cop walked with the grace and femininity of a confident woman, even though her body language indicated that she had wanted to be anywhere but the State Dinner; a consensus that made them comrades.

Before he realized that his feet had moved, Victor was nearing her. Without a slight glance away from the beauty before him, he acknowledged Jeffrey.

"Governor Creed, may I introduce my fiancée, Nicole, and her sister, Taylor Montgomery."

"How lucky you are, Commissioner Morgan, to be accompanied by two of the most beautiful women in the room."

"I'm a very lucky man indeed, Sir," Jeffrey chuckled, standing a bit taller.

Victor nodded toward Jeffrey's fiancée.

"It's so nice to meet you, Governor Creed," she greeted.

"The pleasure is truly mine."

She was a beauty in her own right. Clearly there was some good DNA flowing through the sisters' veins. Victor smiled at her, before devoting his attention to her sister, Taylor. She was a vision. Her natural curls were wild and free, and she looked downright feral, like a beast that could tame him. In nanoseconds,

CREED
by *Phoenix Daniels*

Victor had perused her entire body, before focusing on her beautiful, dark brown, feline-like eyes. He licked his lips before he could stop himself.

Clearing his throat, Victor decided to speak before he did something to really offend the woman.

"It's nice to meet you, Miss Montgomery," he said, as he took her left hand, placing it to his lips. His action was more so to check for a wedding ring. "Welcome to the Executive Mansion."

She smiled as she tugged her hand away. "Thank you, Governor Creed."

"Please call me Victor."

"I couldn't," she said with a chuckle.

"Of course you can," Victor insisted.

She looked around, seemingly taking in the environment. "Everything is so beautiful, Sir."

"Victor," he reiterated. "Maybe I can show you around after dinner?'

"No, Sir," her sister interjected. "We couldn't put you out like that. But thank you."

We? I didn't say shit about 'we'.

Before she'd interrupted, Victor had almost forgotten that the little cock-blocker was in the room.

"Hey, I found our table," a male voice said from behind.

CREED
by *Phoenix Daniels*

Victor turned to find Brent Trainer, the most irritating reporter that he'd ever come across in a press conference. When Brent walked up to Taylor Montgomery and possessively placed his hand in the small of her back, Victor actually stiffened. He stuffed his hands into his pant pockets. He could feel a surge of anger as Brent so freely touched the object of his desire. And the fact that Taylor didn't seem all that comfortable with Brent's gesture didn't exactly give him calm.

"Good evening, Governor," he greeted with an arrogant smirk.

"Trainer," Victor grunted, quickly returning his attention to Taylor.

His eyes narrowed on her as he was mentally warning her to get the reporter's hands off of her. And when she took the subtlest step away from Brent, Victor nodded with a smile as if to say, "Good job."

"Please enjoy your evening," he said, a bit happier, as he walked away.

CREED

by *Phoenix Daniels*

TAYLOR

"I noticed that you can't keep your eyes off of our handsome, single governor," Nicole whispered. "And, apparently, he can't seem to keep his eyes off of you."

Taylor turned to her sister and tried to play dumb. "What are you talking about?"

Nicole pursed her lips and stared pointedly at Taylor. "Girl, stop playing dumb before I slap you."

"I believe you know better than to do that, dear sister," Taylor responded in a sugary tone.

"Whatever. You look so pretty tonight. Although, I wish that you would have worn your hair up."

Taylor stopped herself from rolling her eyes. Nicole could be so overbearing. It wasn't enough that she'd worn the dress and shoes that she'd picked out for her, as if Taylor wasn't capable of putting together her own outfit, but evidently, she didn't believe Taylor could manage her own hair.

Clearly, Nicole was conducting a "find Taylor a man" mission. When Nicole insisted that she tag along with her and her fiancé, Taylor should have known that she was up to something. When she stepped out of her house to find Brent standing by the limo waiting for her, she had to admit that she was a bit surprised

CREED
by *Phoenix Daniels*

by her sister's nerve. Not that Brent wasn't a good-looking man; he was quite handsome in a "beach boy" kind of way. He just didn't seem to be her type. With bouncy blonde hair and striking blue eyes, he'd be considered movie star beautiful. Although very tall, he was a little too lean for Taylor. After all, she wasn't a tiny woman. She was 5'9", which was taller than most women, and nowhere near thin. She knew that she had the kind of curves that she couldn't even begin to hide, even in the bulky uniform that she wore every day. Her mother and her sister were also built as solid as a brick wall. No gust of wind was gonna blow either of them away.

"Seriously, Tay, your hair is so... wild."

"Damn, you're still talking?" Taylor huffed. "I like my hair this way. No, I'm not getting a relaxer. No, I don't need to wear weave. Yours, by the way, is gorgeous, but it's not for me. Why don't you style your hair as you wish, and I'll do the same with mine? And I'll thank you for letting it go."

As exasperating as Nicole was, she was right about one thing; Taylor couldn't keep her eyes off of the good governor of Illinois. He was definitely something to look at. He had a thick mane of silky dark hair framing a gorgeous face and a pair of sultry moss green eyes that seemed to hold promises of erotic nights. And damn if he couldn't fill out a tux. He was a tall, thick

CREED
by *Phoenix Daniels*

piece of eye candy that Taylor would love to unwrap. She knew that he was young and handsome, but television did Governor Creed absolutely no justice. She actually had to hide a shiver when he was standing in front of her. And to make matters worse, Taylor was sure that he was flirting with her. Well, he *was,* until Brent walked up. The governor's entire attitude had changed then. He went from friendly and flirty to almost brooding. Admittedly, the change in his demeanor had stirred something from within Taylor. It was as if she had read his mind. He smiled when she eased from Brent's side. He was visibly pleased, and something about pleasing him made her tingle inside.

"For you," Brent said, handing her a glass of champagne, diverting her attention.

"Thank you."

Taylor smiled and took a less than lady-like gulp, earning her a look of disapproval from Nicole. Taylor shrugged and placed the glass on the table in front of her.

"So, Jeffrey tells me that you're a cop. I'll bet you got some great stories."

"Well, I have stories, but I don't know how great they are."

Brent smiled, showing straight white teeth. "I'm sure that depends on who's listening to them."

CREED
by *Phoenix Daniels*

Taylor retrieved the glass from the table and took a more refined sip before asking, "So, you're a reporter, huh?"

That was her first mistake of the evening, because Brent talked about himself and his "oh so fascinating" stories all through dinner. Even as they danced, Taylor could hear nothing but the incessant ramblings of a man that *really* loved his job. She coped by staring across the ballroom, discreetly eyeing the handsome governor. And when she found the perfect excuse, she politely excused herself.

"Brent, will you excuse me? I think I see an old friend."

"Of course," he responded as he stepped back.

Taylor smiled and took off to the other side of the ballroom. She stopped behind the woman that had caught her attention.

"Victoria Price," Taylor said, prompting the woman to turn around.

"Victoria *Storm*," she corrected with a smile.

"Oh, that's right. I'm still waiting for your tell-all to drop; 'From Streetwalker to Billionaire'."

"Well, keep waiting. I can't teach you tramps all my tricks."

The ladies embraced and laughed together.

"Vic, it's really good to see you. How have you been?"

"Life's good. I got no complaints. You? You still on the job?"

"Yeah, until I meet a millionaire that is," Taylor scoffed.

CREED
by *Phoenix Daniels*

"Looks like your wait is over," Victoria whispered.

Taylor turned and looked over her shoulder. Victoria's husband, Jack Storm, and Governor Creed were standing behind her. They were exceeding the hot guy quota that Taylor thought was in place at stuffy events for the rich. Jack Storm had to be the only man that could pry her eyes away from Victor Creed. And although Jack's unbelievable good looks, charisma, and sex appeal were suffocating, Victor Creed was a god among men. Maybe they were both sons of Zeus.

As Taylor stood before two of the most beautiful men that she'd ever seen, she feared that she'd break out into a sweat at any moment.

"Who's your friend, Sweetheart?" Jack asked.

Damn, his voice is sexy.

"Baby, this is Taylor Montgomery. We were on the department together. Taylor, my husband, Jack, and I trust you know our esteemed governor."

"We've met."

The sexy bass in the governor's voice sent chills down Taylor's spine. She smiled at him, praying that her smile would prompt him to speak again. Jack spoke instead. "Once my wife left the police department, I foolishly thought that they were fresh out of beautiful women. I was terribly wrong."

CREED
by *Phoenix Daniels*

Jack then gently grabbed Taylor's hand and placed it to his lips.

"You're just gonna stand there and watch your husband flirt shamelessly with that beautiful woman?" Victor scolded.

"Leave him be, Governor. He's just having a little fun," Victoria teased.

"Fun my ass," he responded before pulling Taylor's hand from Jack's face.

Victoria giggled at Jack's mischievous smirk, but his smirk immediately disappeared when Brent joined them.

"Mr. Storm, I-" Brent began to say before Jack cut him off.

"There's no story here, Trainer. Get lost."

"Sir, I know that you didn't like the way I reported on your cousin's story, but I was just doing my job."

"Is that so? I guess when a woman is sexually harassed in the workplace, it's your job to attack the character of the victim. Oh, yeah, and I guess you didn't write your story in favor of the police department in order to stay in the good graces of Media Affairs. Trainer, you're an overly ambitious little toad. Go away."

"Actually, Mr. Storm, I'm here to retrieve my lovely date," Brent responded smugly.

Everyone looked at Taylor, causing her to be a bit self-conscious.

CREED
by *Phoenix Daniels*

"Trust me, Gorgeous, you can do better," Jack declared, before walking away.

Hell, Taylor already knew that, and she was thoroughly embarrassed. She'd read the article that Jack had referred to, but had no idea that Brent had written it. It had infuriated her. She knew Natasha Walker from the police academy. She was really shy, and she kept to herself, but the department had tried to destroy her credibility by attacking her character. It was a disgusting turn of events, but that article that described Natasha as a whore was the most disgusting of it all.

"I'm gonna go catch up with Jack," Victoria said, pressing a kiss to her cheek. "I'll catch you later."

"Okay, later," Taylor mumbled.

She turned and nodded toward the governor and walked away, without a word to Brent. But somehow, she knew that he was on her tail.

****

For most of the evening, Taylor had managed to avoid conversing with Brent. She thought it best not to embarrass Nicole and her fiancé by telling Brent just how much of an asshole he was. Ultimately, avoiding a conversation with him was easy, because more than anything, he loved to hear his own

CREED
by *Phoenix Daniels*

voice. So, Taylor happily sat back and let him talk Jeffrey's ear off. As a matter of fact, it was Brent's overblown pride in his accomplishments that had allowed her to sneak away from the table again. After a visit to the ladies' room, Taylor found herself roaming the halls, looking at paintings that she was sure were much older than she was. One caught her eye. It was of a lone, nude woman sitting in a dark forest. It was painted in black and white, with the exception of a throw that was spread over a rock where the woman sat. The throw was painted in a vivid red. Taylor cautiously looked around before lightly touching the canvas.

"It was painted in the late eighteen hundreds by an artistically talented lumberjack that came across a beautiful woman alone in the forest."

The voice caused Taylor to startle. She jumped, removing her hand from the painting.

Damn, it was Brent. Twenty minutes later, he'd finally noticed her absence.

"I finally got you alone."

Taylor looked around the quiet hall. "I guess you do."

He all but groaned. "Whatever will I do with you?"

CREED
by *Phoenix Daniels*

"Nothing. Look, Brent, I'm really not interested in getting involved right now. I didn't know that my sister was going to try and set me up."

"Not interested, huh?" he asked as she stalked toward her. "You seemed very interested when you were creaming your panties for the governor and that asshole, Jack Storm."

"Excuse me?"

Taylor was losing her patience, but he was close enough for her to smell the alcohol on his breath.

"Okay, you're drunk. Let's get you out of here," she said, placing her hand on his arm.

"Are you fucking serious?" he hissed, pulling away. "No, I want you to throw yourself at me, just like you did with those motherfuckers."

With that, he Kung-Fu gripped her ass and pushed his groin against her stomach. Before she knew it, Taylor had performed an armbar that resulted in Brent ending up face down on the floor.

She stepped back, smoothing out the fabric of her dress.

"That's not how you treat a lady." The governor's deep baritone voice rang out in the quiet hall. "I would kick your ass, but it looks like the lady beat me to it. Get up and get your slimy ass out of my house."

CREED
by *Phoenix Daniels*

Brent pulled himself off the floor and fixed his clothes. Just as instructed, he slinked down the hall. Taylor looked over at the governor. He was leaning against a wall with his muscular arms crossed over his chest. His stance was tall and powerful. And when he flashed her a beautiful smile, for the first time, she noticed his dimples.

How can a man that exudes boatloads of power have dimples?

"Governor Creed..."

"Victor."

"Um, okay. Well, Victor, I had it under control."

"I could see that. Truthfully, I could have stood here and watched you kick his ass all night, but I wanted to be alone with you."

"Is that so?"

"Yes, Taylor Montgomery. I've been waiting for the chance all night."

"And now that we're alone?"

Victor flashed a lopsided grin, showing off one adorable dimple. His eyes gleamed with mischief.

"I'd like to invite you to dinner."

His deep, masculine voice washed over her like a warm bath.

CREED
by *Phoenix Daniels*

"Like a date? You can do that?" she asked with a quiver in her voice.

"I'm a man. I like women. Why wouldn't I be able to go on a date?"

"Well, dating a high-profile man could be a bit of a challenge. Let me think about it."

He shook his head. "No, I'm not giving you a chance to talk yourself out of spending time with me. What are your plans for tomorrow?"

"I'm going fishing."

The governor narrowed his eyes and studied Taylor as if to see if she wasn't being truthful. "Fishing? You fish?"

"Yes, sir, I do."

"Where do you fish in Chicago?"

"I don't," Taylor chuckled. "I fish at Fox Lake."

"I see. So, when are you free?"

"Governor, let me check my work schedule. I'll get back to you. I mean... you're the governor, it's not like I don't know where to find you."

The governor seemed to silently contemplate her request. "Ok, get back to me," he relented. He then offered his hand. "Come. I'll escort you back to the party."

CREED
by *Phoenix Daniels*

Taylor placed her hand in his. An instant electric, sexual current flowed between them as he led her back to the ballroom.

CHAPTER 4
TAYLOR

Taylor hopped up from her portable lawn chair and snatched her pole off of the makeshift stand that she'd created from tree limbs. She'd watched the bobble dip into the water, but waited for a good tug on the line.

She had hooked a fish.

She gave the line a good yank, in order to snag the fish, and slowly began to reel it in.

"Yank it again, Small Fry," her dad yelled. "It ain't hooked."

"It's hooked, Daddy. I know what I'm doing."

"You'd better do what your daddy said and yank it again. It'll secure your hold as you reel him in."

Shocked by the voice, Taylor almost dropped her fishing pole. But her dad grabbed her line and gave it a good yank, making it easier for her to reel it in. Taylor was excited about the size of the Rainbow Trout that she'd caught as it broke through the surface. She grabbed the line and held up the big fish with pride as her dad, along with Governor Creed, clapped for her achievement.

"What are you doing here?" she asked Victor when the clapping ended.

CREED

by *Phoenix Daniels*

"I came to fish. I like fishing," he responded with an innocent shrug.

Taylor shook her head and kneeled to remove her catch from the hook.

"Daddy, this is-"

"Small Fry, do you think that I'm so ignorant that I wouldn't recognize the governor of Illinois?"

"Daddy, I was just trying to be polite," Taylor giggled.

"Governor Creed, this is my dad, James Montgomery."

The governor, with his eyes narrowed at Taylor for not referring to him as Victor, extended his hand.

"It's nice to meet you, Mr. Montgomery. Please call me Victor."

Her dad shook his outstretched hand and responded. "Only if you call me James."

"Yes, sir."

"So, I'm assuming you're here because you're sniffing around my little girl."

Victor's eyes widened. Visibly thrown off by James' assumption, he cleared his throat and responded.

"Um... yes. Yes, sir, I guess I am."

"All right. Well, I'll be back. I gotta go see a man about a dog."

CREED

by *Phoenix Daniels*

Taylor gawked at both her dad and the governor. They were both blowing her mind; the governor for ambushing her fishing trip, and her dad for bailing out so easily.

When her dad walked away, she stared pointedly at the governor.

"Governor Creed, I'm really confused as to why you're here right now. Did you really come here to fish with me?"

"Yes, and I'm really confused as to why you refuse to call me Victor."

"Because you're the governor."

"And you're a police officer. Do you prefer to be called Officer Montgomery when you're not on duty?"

"No, but, it's a little different for me."

"Please, call me Victor."

"Okay, Victor," Taylor acquiesced with a smile. She was more comfortable being on a first-name basis with him than she thought she'd be.

"Thank you, Taylor. Now, may I fish with you guys? I don't get to do this much."

Taylor perused his attire. He was wearing a gray t-shirt, Timberland boots, and holding a fishing pole. He came prepared to fish, and had it not been for the huge security detail standing in the trees, he almost seemed like a normal guy.

CREED
by *Phoenix Daniels*

Taylor opened a small Styrofoam cooler. "Pick your bait."

CREED

Although he hadn't expected to meet her father, fishing with the two of them reminded Victor of the fun that he used to have before he began a life of politics. He admired, almost envied, the easy way that Taylor and James interacted. His relationship with his father was far more formal. Victor and his father had been fishing, golfing, and other things, but their activities were always tied to some sort of business deal or political move. But as he observed father and daughter, it was clear that they simply enjoyed spending time together. They were fun and playful, sincerely enjoying each other's company. They had something that was special and just for the two of them.

If Victor was intruding on their bonding time, they hadn't made him feel like it. Not one time did they make him feel unwanted. In fact, they had embarked on a friendly competition, in which James was winning by a landslide. He'd caught four, Taylor two, but James was on his seventh catch.

Tearing his eyes away from Taylor was another challenge in itself. She was beautiful without effort. Even with no makeup and her hair in a wild bushy ponytail, she so easily put so many

CREED
by *Phoenix Daniels*

women to shame. Her skin was flawless. Her lips were full and luscious. Her exotic eyes had the ability to hypnotize any man that dared to look too long. And her body... so voluptuous that the dirty white t-shirt and ragged jeans were sexier than any piece of lingerie. Taylor was surely a tomboy, and Victor had never been attracted to that type. But she'd definitely changed his perspective. He wanted her; bad. Yet, the more time he spent with her, he wondered exactly what it was that he wanted from her.

At the end of the evening, when the fish were sleeping, and the mosquitoes were feasting on their flesh, Victor helped James and Taylor load their equipment into the back of James' pickup. Victor wasn't ready for his time with Taylor to end, so he walked over to her dad and asked, "James, sir, is it okay if I see Taylor home?"

"Well, young man, that's entirely up to Taylor."

"Yes, Victor," Taylor intervened. "That would've been my decision to make."

Victor walked around the bed of the truck and leaned into her.

"I was simply trying to be respectful. I didn't mean to be presumptuous. I planned to ask you as well."

"I know and thank you, but it's quite a drive back. I don't want my dad to have to make that drive alone."

CREED
by *Phoenix Daniels*

"Nonsense, Small Fry. I can make that drive with my eyes closed."

"Sir, I wouldn't recommend that," Victor chuckled.

"Gone on, y'all," James said with a wave of his hand. "Drive safe."

With that, he climbed into his pickup and started the engine. Taylor jogged to the driver's side, leaned in the window, and kissed her dad's cheek.

"Call me when you get home," she told him.

"Will do."

"Okay, Daddy. Love you."

"Me too."

With that said, he shifted into drive and took off down the road. Taylor watched for a few seconds and then turned to Victor. "Well, I'm all yours."

"Not yet, but you will be," he responded with a devilishly sexy smirk.

Taylor smiled, and if she was the least bit offended by his comment, she hadn't shown it. Victor had plans to taste every part of her body, and maybe she was coming to terms with that.

CREED

by *Phoenix Daniels*

TAYLOR

Taylor sat next to Victor in the back of the SUV and watched him as he attempted to field, what seemed like, hundreds of calls while attempting to have a conversation with her.

Damn, it's Sunday. His life is truly hectic.

Taylor wondered how he managed to sit on a bank with her and her father for so long without his phone ringing even once. When he ended his last call, he turned to Taylor and smiled sympathetically, before dialing another number. After a few seconds, he spoke into the phone, "Kena, handle my calls. I'll call you when I'm back in rotation."

He ended the call and turned to face her. The intensity in his stare caused Taylor to feel a tiny bit self-conscious.

"What?" she asked, forcing herself to maintain eye contact.

"You're absolutely beautiful, Taylor; so completely and naturally beautiful."

"Thank you, Victor," she responded, exhaling a breath that she didn't know that she was holding. The truth was, when he looked at her with such intensity, it took her to another place.

"I gotta tell you, Victor, this is really weird," she admitted.

CREED
by *Phoenix Daniels*

Victor placed his hand over hers. "I know, but I'd really like to see you again." His response was filled with sincerity. "May I have your phone number so that I can call you?"

He grabbed something from the door of the SUV. Taylor realized that he was handing her a business card.

"This is my personal cellular number and my office number. Call me anytime."

Taylor took a quick peek at the card and stuffed it into her back pocket. "You can put my number in your phone."

After storing her number in his phone, Victor tossed it on the seat. Taylor glanced down at his hand that covered hers. The sparks between them were so powerful that she looked to see if the current would actually be visible to the naked eye. With his other hand, he gently ran his thumb across her cheek.

"Have dinner with me tomorrow," he said in a voice that was demanding, but oh so sensual. "I won't take no for an answer."

"You'll have to because I have to work tomorrow night," she said with more regret than she expected.

"What time do you get off?"

"Midnight."

"Damn. So, when are you off?"

"Thursday."

"I suppose I can wait 'til Thursday."

CREED
by *Phoenix Daniels*

"Now, how do you know that I didn't already have plans?"

"Young lady, I'm the governor. Don't make me throw my weight around."

"Okay," she chuckled. "Thursday it is."

"Good. I'll call you to finalize."

Taylor nodded her response without looking away from his beautiful olive eyes. For the first time, she noticed light specs of hazel.

"We're here."

She was so mesmerized that she hadn't even noticed that they had pulled into her driveway. He gave her hand a light squeeze, saying, "Come. Let me walk you to the door."

"Okay," she mumbled as she gathered her things.

Admittedly, she was disappointed that their time together was over.

When the door was opened, Victor stepped out and extended his hand to her. She placed her hand in his, and their electrical spark was reignited. He helped her from the vehicle and closed the door. He placed his hand in the small of her back and led her up the walkway. Halfway to the front door, he turned to tell one of his shadows to fall back. He held her hand as they walked up the steps of her porch.

"Nice house. It's pretty big, though. You live here alone?"

CREED
by *Phoenix Daniels*

"Yep. It's just me," she responded while digging her keys out of her purse.

She unlocked the door and turned to say goodnight. But, before she could speak, he placed his hands on both sides of her face and guided her face to his. When his lips connected with hers, Taylor literally went weak in the knees. She grasped his upper arms in order to stay on her feet. She wrapped her fingers around his muscular biceps as he made love to her mouth. As his tongue caressed hers, her body melded to his. He was literally sucking her in, and Taylor knew that she would never forget the kiss that she shared with the governor of Illinois.

CREED
by *Phoenix Daniels*

CHAPTER 5
TAYLOR

Three days later, Taylor was still fantasizing about the kiss that she shared with Victor. As she lay in bed the night before, she could still feel his lips on hers, his tongue teasing hers. She could practically feel the vibrations as he moaned softly into her mouth. Victor had invaded her thoughts for the last three days.

He was still invading them when Taylor heard the dispatcher's voice blaring in her ear. "2234?"

Taylor reached for the radio on her shoulder strap. "2234. What's up, squad?"

"There's a call of a domestic disturbance. Wife says the husband hit her, and he won't leave."

After the dispatcher read out the address, Taylor responded with, "10-4. En route."

"Do you need backup?" asked the dispatcher.

"We'll let you know. We're three blocks away."

"10-4."

Maria sped up. After turning a few corners, she pulled over close to the address that was dispatched. Taylor stepped out of the squad car and assessed her surroundings. It was quiet. Whatever the disturbance was, it was contained indoors.

CREED
by *Phoenix Daniels*

Taylor flanked by Maria, approached the house cautiously, and knocked on the door. After a few seconds, the door flew open, and a young woman appeared. She couldn't have been any more than twenty-five years old. She had a panicked expression, and there was blood trickling from her mouth.

"He's in the bedroom," she said in a hushed voice, pointing to a closed door down a hall.

The woman stepped out of the way to allow them inside.

"Stay here," Maria told the woman as they cautiously made their way to the bedroom.

Taylor looked around the almost-empty house. In the living room, there was a beat-up couch and a television that was sitting on top of milk crates. Once at the end of the hall, Taylor turned the knob and slowly opened the door. Soon they had an unobstructed view of a six foot five inch, butt naked man. The smirk on his face was proof that his intention was to use his nudity as a distraction.

Under any other circumstance, it would have worked. He was a fairly attractive, muscular man.

"Sir, we got a call. Did you hit your wife?" Maria asked.

"What goes on between a man and his wife is none of your business. Now, unless you're planning on sucking my dick, get the fuck out of my house," hissed the naked man.

CREED
by *Phoenix Daniels*

"2234," Taylor called into her radio.

"Go, 2234."

"Roll us another car over here."

"10-4. We'll get you some backup."

Taylor and Maria triangulated the bigger man. Maria's hand migrated toward her pepper spray, as opposed to Taylor's, that inched toward her asp.

"Get the fuck out of my house!" the man bellowed, bolting toward them.

Taylor flung the asp to its full length and swung as if she was teeing off on a golf course, delivering a painful blow to the man's genitals. The woman beater fell on all fours. Before he could recover, Maria blinded him by spraying a good amount of pepper spray in his face. As he wailed loudly, Taylor thought to herself that no grown man his size should be screaming like a little bitch. However, though most abusers can dish out pain, but they can't take it.

Suddenly, the so-called victim entered the room screaming, "What are you doing to him?! Stop! You're hurting him!"

Is this bitch serious?

Taylor took a second to look back at the stupid woman. Her lip was still bleeding, and it had tripled in size. She yelled at the woman to get out and returned her attention to the immediate threat. Taylor used the asp to sweep his hands from under him. When he fell face down, they pounced. It was a struggle, but they'd finally got his hands behind his back so that Maria could slip on the handcuffs. Once his hands were secure, they dragged the man from the bedroom. The pepper spray in the small room was beginning to affect their vision and breathing.

Taylor could hear sirens approach and the sound of screeching tires once they entered the living room. Since the offender was cuffed and ass naked, he was assumed secure and without weapons, so she leaned against the wall and coughed in between deep breaths, attempting to clear the pepper spray from her lungs. Maria did the same.

Taylor pushed off the wall when she heard the heavy footsteps of her fellow officers storming the front porch. She grabbed the radio on her shoulder and called for the dispatcher.

"Squad, you can slow it down. The offender is in custody."

"10-4."

The dispatcher informed the other officers, who were en route to provide backup, that the scene was secure. She thanked them for responding and instructed them that backup was no longer needed.

"2234?" the dispatcher called.

"2234. Go."

CREED
by *Phoenix Daniels*

"Your victim requested a supervisor. Sergeant Howard is en route."

"10-4, Squad. Thanks."

Taylor looked up at Maria, who was shaking her head. Before either could comment, several officers entered the living room.

"Well, he is a big one," Corey Campbell commented. "But y'all don't look like ya needed no help."

"What you mean, Corey? We'll always need you and your big strong arms for protection," Maria responded, flirtatiously.

"Cut it out, Mendez!" Sergeant Howard interrupted. "You can work on committing adultery when you get off the clock."

Taylor laughed and asked, "What's the deal, Sarge?"

"Don't know. I'll let you know when I do. Campbell, get this dude in the wagon."

Corey nodded and lifted the big naked man off the floor. He then turned to Taylor, saying, "Bring something for this motherfucker to put on when you come out."

Sergeant Howard shook his head in disgust as Corey and his partner escorted the blind, naked man out of the house. Then he walked over to the battered woman, and before he could ask her one question, she announced, "I'm the one that called."

"What's the problem?" Sgt. Howard asked in a dry tone.

CREED

by *Phoenix Daniels*

"These officers!" she shouted. "They used excessive force on my husband, and I want to file a complaint."

With furrowed brows, Sgt. Howard stared at the young woman.

"You want to file a complaint against these officers that you called to stop your husband from beating your ass? Is that correct?"

"They didn't have to beat him like that."

"Well, ma'am, unlike you, he doesn't have a mark on him. But I'll tell you what; I'm gonna take your complaint, and then I'm gonna have my officers release your husband so that he can come in here and kick your ass for calling the police on him in the first place. Would that suffice?"

Fear washed over her face as she contemplated the sergeant's, not so veiled, threat. She placed her hand to her chest and said, "Never mind. Take him."

"Sure, as soon as you thank my officers for saving your ass."

"Thank you," she mumbled with a roll of her eyes.

"Go get some clothes for him," Maria responded, without grace.

She walked into the bedroom without another word.

"I'm out," Sergeant Howard said over his shoulder as he left the house.

CREED
by *Phoenix Daniels*

Maria started to giggle, causing Taylor to look over at her.

"What?" Taylor asked.

"Girl, did you see the size of that anaconda? No wonder her ass ain't left." Then she whispered, "Hell, if Mike had a dick that big, I'll let him smack me around every now and then."

"Girl, bye," Taylor chuckled. "The first time Mike hit yo' ass, you gonna Lorena Bobbitt that motherfucker."

"I know, right?" Maria admitted. "Tell that bitch to hurry up so we can go."

No sooner than Maria spoke the words, the lady entered the living room with a bag of clothing. Taylor took the bag, and they both exited the ungrateful woman's house.

Once they reentered their squad car, Taylor called the dispatcher. "2234."

"2234?" the dispatcher responded.

"We're going to the station with one arrest. Thank everyone for the backup."

"Going into the station," she repeated. "10-4."

CREED

by *Phoenix Daniels*

CREED

Since the NATO summit was to be held in Chicago this year, Victor was sitting through yet another prep meeting. Present was Charles Buchanan, the lieutenant governor, and Carl Rountree, the mayor of Chicago. Chicago's police superintendent and the deputy superintendent were also present, along with FBI intelligence. The NATO summit would require a number of the Heads of State and the Heads of Government of NATO countries to convene in one place. Therefore, law enforcement was essential. There were bound to be a number of protests and even more threats of terrorism. So, Victor knew just how important every prep meeting was, but that didn't stop his thoughts from drifting to Taylor. He couldn't wait to see her again, to kiss her again. He reminisced about the way she submitted completely to him when he kissed her. He imagined her submitting her entire beautiful body to him. Surprisingly, he found himself daydreaming of doing things other than sex with her. He could see them fishing and hunting together. Hell, he wished he could take walks with her or even hold her hand in a movie theater. She was so beautiful that he actually wanted to sleep next to her just to see how beautiful she was in the morning. Damn, Taylor

CREED
by *Phoenix Daniels*

Montgomery had bewitched him. She was just so different from any woman that he'd ever met.

Victor was so lost in his thoughts that he hadn't even noticed that his meeting had come to an end. He remained at the head of the conference table and watched everyone file out of the room. He rubbed his chin and wondered what to plan for his date with Taylor. Admittedly, dating was difficult for him, and dating Taylor, a "normal" woman, was really going to be a challenge. Would she understand that he couldn't just walk into a restaurant, hand-in-hand with a woman like the average man? Since he'd lost his wife, every woman that he'd been with had understood his limitations as governor, but Taylor was different. She was special. And he had actually considered publicly dating her, but he needed to know how she felt about being linked to him first.

Victor fished his phone from his jacket pocket and dialed Taylor's number.

"Hello?" The sexy rasp in her voice sent a wake-up signal straight to his cock.

"Hello, gorgeous."

"How are you, Governor Creed?" Victor could hear the smile in her voice.

"I'm just fine, Officer Montgomery. How are you?"

"I'm good. What's up?"

CREED
by *Phoenix Daniels*

"Well, about our date tomorrow; how do you feel about, instead of going out, having dinner at my apartment in Chicago?"

"I feel just fine about that, sir."

"Good, I'll send a car for you at seven."

"I can drive."

"Yes, I know. *A car will be there at seven.*"

"Yes, sir," she chuckled.

"Good. Now that that's settled, how was your day?"

Victor's hectic day was finally coming to a pleasant end as he laughed and talked with her for thirty minutes. Her wit and easy-going nature were a breath of fresh air in a polluted world. He'd found himself still smiling, even after their call had ended. He was so enamored that he hadn't noticed that he wasn't alone in the large conference room.

"So, you have a hot date? How sweet, Governor Creed."

Victor closed his eyes and stilled himself for a few seconds before turning to face Kara Edwards. Her presence wasn't a surprise. As his press secretary, she roamed freely through the Thompson Center.

"Kara, hello."

"So, you dump me, and, in a flash, you're on to someone new."

CREED
by *Phoenix Daniels*

"Kara, you knew going in that I wasn't looking for anything long term, and you assured me that you weren't either."

"So, you, and only you, get to decide when the term has ended?"

"Kara, I-"

"Who in the fuck is Taylor?!" she screamed.

Victor stared at the woman, who had used him for sex for months while screaming from the rooftop that she could handle a strictly physical relationship.

He buttoned his suit coat and prepared to exit the conference room. "Taylor..." he responded, coolly, "...is none of your business. Your business is handling the media on my behalf. Are you going to able to handle your *actual* business, Kara?"

Without waiting for an answer, he walked out of the conference room, leaving her seething.

As far as Victor was concerned, that conversation was over forever.

CREED
by *Phoenix Daniels*

CHAPTER 6
TAYLOR

Taylor picked a piece of lint off of her black pencil skirt, wondering if she should have chosen a different outfit. She'd paired it with a green silk blouse. Once the town car came to a stop, she stopped fidgeting and gawked at the massive building. Once the door was opened, the driver assisted her from the car.

"Thank you," she said in almost a whisper, still staring up at the impressive piece of real estate. Taylor had only ever seen Storm Tower from the expressway. The building was a significant part of Chicago's beautiful skyline.

"You're welcome, Miss Montgomery."

The driver's use of her name prompted Taylor to look at him.

"What's your name?" she asked him.

"I'm Collier, ma'am; the governor's regular driver."

"But you're driving me. So, what happens if there's an emergency and the governor needed to be mobile?"

"There are backups in place, ma'am," he chuckled.

"Well, it's nice to meet you, Collier."

"And you, ma'am. This way please," he said with his hand stretched toward the entrance. "I'm to escort you up."

"Thank you. And please call me Taylor."

CREED
by *Phoenix Daniels*

"Yes, ma'am," he responded.

Taylor chuckled and followed him inside. As they walked through the lobby, Collier nodded to more security personnel. They nodded in return and glanced curiously at Taylor. She simply smiled and kept walking.

Once they were in the elevator, Collier pushed P88, the button for the penthouse on the eighty-eighth floor. They rode in silence, but it wasn't awkward. She was grateful for the silence. Admittedly, Taylor was a bit nervous. This was no average date, and Victor Creed was no average man.

When the elevator arrived at the desired floor, the doors glided open and revealed an awaiting Victor. He stood tall and unbelievably handsome. His towering stature and big body made her feel tiny. He was wearing a blue dress shirt with no tie and dark slacks. It was an easygoing look for the normally well-kept governor. Even his thick wavy hair was styled in a more relaxed fashion. Taylor glanced at the full lips that had kissed her with such enormous passion and mused that they were really plump for a white man.

"Hello, beautiful," he greeted with a smirk.

"Hey," Taylor responded.

She smiled and stepped off the elevator.

CREED

by *Phoenix Daniels*

"Thank you, Collier," Victor said over her shoulder just as the doors slid closed.

Victor pulled her into his arms and kissed the top of her head.

"I'm glad you could make it," he said against her hair.

"Me too."

"Ma'am, I need to search your bag," said a voice coming from behind Victor.

Taylor looked around Victor's broad shoulders. She hadn't even noticed the large man in a dark suit leaning on a wall across from the elevator.

"I don't think so, mister," she responded in a calm tone, instinctively gripping her purse.

"Ma'am," he pressed, pushing off the wall.

"Sir, do you have a weapon?"

"Yes, ma'am I do."

"And it's your job to protect him?" she asked, pointing to Victor.

"It is."

"Well, sir, I have a weapon as well, and it's my job to protect me."

Victor seemed amused by the back and forth between her and the bigger man, but Taylor wasn't amused at all. She didn't like relinquishing her weapon. But the announcement of the

CREED
by *Phoenix Daniels*

weapon in her possession caused the bodyguard to close the distance between them. Victor placed himself between them and held his hand up, halting the bodyguard.

"Gregor, she's a cop," he told him.

Taylor could tell that the bodyguard couldn't have cared less.

"Taylor, sweetheart, give him your bag." She turned to Victor with narrowed eyes, but before she could respond, he added, "It's his job. Besides, I'm here to protect you."

He flashed his charming smile, revealing perfect white teeth. Taylor reluctantly handed the man her purse. Victor was irresistible. He could probably convince her to rob a bank with just his smile, compounded with that rich, sexy baritone.

The guard, meticulously, searched her purse. He pulled her pistol out of the bag and tucked it into his pant pocket. He returned her purse and said, "Ma'am, you can have your firearm back once you leave."

Taylor swallowed her unease and nodded. Victor was right. The man was just doing his job. Hell, Victor was the governor, after all. Of course, security would be tight.

"I'm sorry," she told the guard. "I'm not used to giving up Nina Boo."

"Nina Boo?" he asked, confused.

"That's her name."

CREED
by *Phoenix Daniels*

He was amused. "You named your weapon?"

"Yep," Taylor confirmed.

"Well, Nina Boo..." he reassured, patting his pocket. "... will be waiting right here for you."

"All right, Gregor, stop flirting with my lady," Victor said as he placed a possessive arm around Taylor and led them into a penthouse, leaving Gregor in the hall laughing.

"Oh my God," Taylor gasped when she stepped into the penthouse.

It was a grandiose palace that was impeccably designed. It had an open layout with curved lines. There was a remarkable panoramic view of the city. The walls were bright white and covered with art that could have dated back to the 17th Century.

"Wow, Governor Creed, with your salary being public record and all, I know damn well you can't afford this place. The bribery business must be very lucrative," she jested.

"Hey, don't make jokes like that. The governors of Illinois have a tendency to wind up in prison."

Taylor realized that he was right and burst into laughter. "Sorry… This is a nice place, though."

"Thank you. And I'll have you know that before I became the governor of the great state of Illinois, I owned a very lucrative business."

CREED
by *Phoenix Daniels*

"Oh, is that so?"

"Yes. Maybe you've heard of it; Opulent Cruises."

Taylor's eyes got big. "Not only have I heard of it, but I've also traveled to the Caribbean on one of your cruise liners."

"Please tell me that you loved it and had the time of your life."

"Well, Governor Creed, I loved every minute of it and had the time of my life," Taylor giggled.

"Seriously?"

"Yep, had a ball."

"Good to know my little brothers aren't running our business into the ground."

Taylor had seen pictures of Victor's brothers during his campaign. There were four of them total, and they were just as tall and almost as good looking as Victor. The handsome young brothers were media favorites.

Victor placed his hand in the small of her back and led her to the sofa, asking, "Would you like a drink?"

"What do you have?"

"Everything," he chuckled.

"Okay, then I'll have a Grey Goose and tonic."

"Lime?'

"Of course."

CREED
by *Phoenix Daniels*

"I have to go and check on the food. I'll be back with your drink."

He headed toward what she guessed was the kitchen.

"Whoa, wait, you cooked?"

"I did," he responded over his shoulder.

Although impressed, Taylor didn't comment. However, she did sneak a peek at his tight muscular ass.

CREED

by *Phoenix Daniels*

CREED

Taylor removed the napkin from her lap and placed it on the table. Victor hadn't taken his eyes off of her the entire evening. From the time the elevator doors opened, and she appeared in front of him, it was over for Victor. He was done in. She was wearing a green blouse that all but groped her full tits. There was a respectful amount of cleavage, but not enough to stifle his imagination. He was picturing himself cupping her heavy tits as she rode his cock. And that tight skirt… damn; it was hugging her hips in a way that Victor had never seen. He wanted her, wanted to skip dinner and take her straight to bed. He couldn't keep his eyes off of her. And her hair, so wild and beautiful, was the icing on the cake. Taylor was alluring, and he simply couldn't look away. He hadn't even tried.

"Victor, dinner was amazing. I can't believe that you cook that well."

"Thank you. My mother insisted that my brothers and I learned to cook."

"Well, thank you, Momma Creed. The seafood pasta was amazing."

Victor did a subtle bow. "I gotta say, watching you eat was a refreshing experience. Most women eat like birds when they

CREED
by *Phoenix Daniels*

think someone is watching. But you seemed to really appreciate a good meal."

"Don't try to feed me if you don't want me to eat," she chuckled.

Victor laughed and tossed his napkin on the table.

"Victor, as you can see, I'm not exactly frail," she said with a wave over herself.

"Frail? No, not frail. Beautiful, sexy, curvy, and voluptuous. Yes, a fucking bombshell is what I see."

Victor stood and pulled her from her chair. He pulled her body close to his and wrapped his arms around her waist. Pleased when her arms circled his neck, he pushed his body against her. His cock was so hard that it would be impossible for Taylor not to feel it. When she didn't pull away, he whispered, "This is what your lack of frailty does to me, Taylor."

She looked up at him with fire blazing in her eyes. "What else does it do to you?" she asked in a wanton voice.

"Mmm, baby, so much," Victor respond, pushing his erection against her.

When she ran her fingers through his hair and massaged his scalp, Victor couldn't contain his excitement. He was going to have her.

CREED
by *Phoenix Daniels*

He gripped her round ass and slammed his lips against hers. He licked the seam of her mouth, coaxing her lips apart. She smelled of lime, and he wanted to know if she tasted the same.

Taylor, apparently, had wanted to taste him as well. She pulled slightly away, slowing his advance, and ran her tongue seductively over his lips before sucking his bottom lip into her warm mouth. His cock began to pulse and strain against his zipper. That was it for Victor. He tightened his grip on her ass and lifted her from the floor. His plan was to walk her into the nearest bedroom. He didn't want her on the couch. He intended to worship every inch of her body.

But they were interrupted.

"Governor Creed, I'm sorry to interrupt, but-" Kenyatta started.

"Then don't!" Victor grunted harshly against Taylor's mouth.

His irritation at the interruption grew when Taylor wiggled out of his arms to stand on her own.

"I'm sorry, Governor, but it can't be helped," Kenyatta insisted.

She had walked into the dining room. She was standing her ground. At that point, Victor was sure that whatever it was, was serious. Kenyatta would never have been so bold and intrusive.

CREED
by *Phoenix Daniels*

He turned to Taylor. "Sweetheart, please have a seat. Make yourself at home, and I'll be right back."

"Um, I can go if-" she started.

Taylor leaving was the last thing that Victor wanted. "No, don't go. I'll be right back."

"No, sir, you won't. I'm sorry," Kenyatta contradicted. She then turned to Taylor. "Officer Montgomery, I really apologize for the interruption."

"It's ok, Miss..."

"Kena. Call me Kena, please. I'm the governor's PA. Again, I'm very sorry for the interruption."

"It's fine, Kena. I should be going anyway."

Victor stood by in disbelief. Taylor was leaving. Kenyatta had just waltzed into his dining room and poured cold water on his hot date.

"I'll walk you out," he told Taylor.

As the two of them walked past Kena, Victor said through gritted teeth, "There had better be the threat of a dirty bomb somewhere in Illinois. *In Illinois!* If it's in Indiana, you're fired. If it's in Wisconsin, you're fired."

Kena nodded. "Yes, sir."

"Let Collier know that Miss Montgomery is on her way down."

CREED
by *Phoenix Daniels*

"Done, sir."

Victor placed his hand in the small of Taylor's back in order to regain their physical connection. He stopped her at the front door and turned her to face him. "To be continued?" he asked hopefully.

She smiled. "I can't wait."

Victor breathed a sigh of relief and captured her face in his hands. He kissed her gently on the lips before opening the door and watching her walk away. He stood in the doorway and watched as Gregor turned over her weapon and pushed the call button. When the elevator arrived, she stepped in and turned toward Victor.

"Thanks for dinner," she said, just as the doors closed.

She was gone, and Victor couldn't help but to feel a loss. He didn't believe that he'd ever wanted a woman so bad. His dick was rock hard. He felt an unusual connection, and he couldn't figure out what made Taylor Montgomery so different. But, for now, figuring Taylor out would have to wait. He slammed the door and stormed into the dining room.

"What the fuck, Kena?!"

"Mmmm, you watch your tone with me, Governor Creed. I didn't create this mess."

CREED

by *Phoenix Daniels*

Victor took a deep breath and calmed himself before asking, "What mess, Kenyatta?"

"Kara Edwards. She tried to hang herself in your Chicago office," Kena blurted, rather unsympathetically, in Victor's opinion.

"Are you serious?" he asked with narrowed eyes, sure that Kena was fucking with him.

"As a heart attack. She was found hanging from the ceiling fan in your office."

"Oh, God! What the hell?" Victor shouted, running his fingers roughly through his hair.

"She's alive," Kena murmured.

"Kenyatta! Honestly, you sound disappointed," Victor responded in disbelief.

"That conniving little bi-"

"Kena!"

"She was never in any danger of dying."

"What do you mean?" Victor asked, confused.

"Well, for one, there was a mysterious call to security by an anonymous female caller stating that they believed that your office was being burglarized. And two, she wrote a four-page suicide letter that spoke of her relationship with you... in the future."

CREED
by *Phoenix Daniels*

"So.... you're saying...?"

"She's a public relations guru. She knew exactly what she was doing. I handled it."

Victor's eyes narrowed in suspicion. "What do you mean, you handled it?" he asked, gesturing quotation marks with his fingers.

"I made sure that no one dialed 911. I called a physician to your office. There won't be any hospital records, and I burned that fucking love letter that she called a suicide note."

"Okay, good job. So, if you did all that, why are you here?"

Kena took an impatient breath and blew it out. "Kara is threatening to admit herself into a hospital and tell the press that your cruelty toward her pushed her to attempt suicide, if you don't go and talk to her."

Victor closed his eyes and ran his fingers roughly through his hair. He opened his eyes to find Kenyatta, with her arms folded, awaiting a solution. He paced the floor a few times and turned back to his assistant.

"Tell her that I'm unavailable and to do what she has to do."

"But, Gov-"

"No, Kena, I won't be blackmailed. Besides, Kara's no fool. She loves her career more than anything. She's been busting down doors for years to get where she is. Kara would lose every bit of credibility if our affair came out."

"Are you sure?"

"Yes, I'm sure" he responded with conviction

Kenyatta nodded with a whisper of a smile. She clearly approved. "I'll handle it."

"Thank you, Kena."

"You're welcome. Goodnight, Governor."

"Goodnight," Victor sighed.

CREED

by *Phoenix Daniels*

TAYLOR

Taylor locked the front door and kicked off her heels. She could hardly believe how aroused she was when she left Victor's apartment. She had all but thrown her pussy at him. She wished that she could blame it on the vodka tonics, but she'd only had one. If his assistant hadn't interrupted, she would have been biting his pillow in a matter of minutes.

She unbuttoned her blouse as she walked into the kitchen. The rest of her evening had been decided. It was definitely gonna be a cold shower, buzzing Rabbit kind of night. She poured herself a glass of wine, grabbed the bottle, and headed to her bedroom. No sooner than she'd sat the pair down on her nightstand did the she hear the doorbell. Taylor looked at the cable box; it was nearing ten o'clock. She hurried down the hall and peeked out of the living room window. There were dark vehicles lining the curb. She went to the front door when the bell rang again.

"Who is it?" she shouted through the door.

"It's me, Victor."

After the very abrupt interruption from earlier, she was sure that something horrible had happened, so she yanked the door open. Apparently, Taylor was in a tizzy for no reason because

CREED
by *Phoenix Daniels*

Victor was smiling, and rather seductively. Only when hit by a breeze did Taylor realize that her blouse was still open. She was unintentionally flashing Victor and his entire security detail. Thank God she was wearing her "I might get laid" underwear.

"So beautiful," he whispered.

She crossed her arms over her chest and stepped out of the doorway. Victor stepped inside and closed the door.

"Victor, is everything okay?"

"It will be," he said, closing the distance between them.

He gently eased her hands away from her chest and led them slowly down his torso until they reached the bulge in his pants. Taylor closed her eyes and gasped at the sheer size of him.

"Help me make it okay, Taylor," he whispered while peppering sweet kisses on her neck.

Her body warmed as he ignited flames from within. A moan escaped her lips as she massaged his package, determined to make it okay.

"Victor," she whispered, just before he took her lips.

His kiss was no longer gentle, but urgent. His pace was less than steady as he slid her blouse down her arms and lowered himself enough to lick the cleavage expelling from her lace bra. Her pussy clenched uncontrollably as moisture pooled in her core. Her fingers caressed his head as he mastered the zipper of

CREED
by *Phoenix Daniels*

her skirt and peeled it down her hips, kissing her torso along the way. Taylor stepped out of her skirt and allowed him to lead her to the sofa, where he sat her down gently. Victor lowered to his knees before her and spread her thighs. Taylor was certain that he could feel the heat emanating from her insides. She was so hot and so wet that her panties were pasted to her sex. Even though he was kneeling in front of her, he still was too far. Taylor reached out for him. She was desperate for his touch. As if reading her mind, he lowered his mouth to hers and plunged his tongue inside. His touch, his taste, the aroma of masculinity left Taylor no other alternative than to surrender to the fever as she squirmed beneath him. She wrapped her arms around his solid body, pulling him as close as possible. In a frenzy, she ground her pussy against his dick, in an attempt to douse the flames. Her breathing quickened, and her heart raced as she worked vigorously against his crotch.

"Mmm, Taylor, you're going to be my undoing," Victor growled.

He made quick work of removing her bra. When her breasts sprang free, Taylor excited as his gaze roamed over her with appreciation.

"So beautiful," he whispered as he palmed both breasts.

CREED
by *Phoenix Daniels*

Taylor whimpered with desperation when he sucked her pebbled nipple into his hot mouth. Powerful currents shot to her sex as he licked and sucked the sensitive bud. So frantic, she found herself grinding against air.

"Victor, fuck me, please," she begged.

Without releasing her nipple, he slid his fingers into the crotch of her dampened panties. He rubbed her swollen clit, causing her to cry out. With no warning, Victor ripped the thin material from her body. He grabbed her hips and pulled her to the very edge of the sofa, before plunging between her thighs. He licked her entire pussy before sucking her throbbing clit between his lips, confirming his own pleasure with a sensual moan.

"Ohh, fuck!" Taylor shouted. "Ohh! Ugh!"

Taylor found herself on the brink of insanity as he licked, sucked, and gorged on her. And when he inserted a thick finger, her pussy clenched and she lost control, exploding around it. Taylor froze as wave after wave of ecstasy rolled through her. But Victor wasn't finished. He continued to lick her throbbing center, causing her entire body to shake uncontrollably. The sensation was becoming too much for Taylor to handle, so much so that she actually pushed against his forehead as a plea for mercy. When he relented, she exhaled a breath that she had been painfully holding.

CREED
by *Phoenix Daniels*

Victor stood, still fully clothed. Taylor admired his large dick, stretching the fabric of his pants. As he undressed, she tried to control her breathing and still her quivering body. But when he was fully naked, the sight of his chiseled form and steel-hard dick did nothing to calm her. Taylor licked her lips and marveled at his manhood. The size of it was damn near threatening. And he knew it because when Taylor looked up at him, he was donning a smirk that was almost arrogant. He began to slowly stroke the length of his dick. The erotic scene caused Taylor's mouth to water. She moved closer, intending to take him into her mouth, but he halted her progression with a hand to her shoulder.

"Next time, baby. I need to be inside of you," he said in a deep hoarse voice.

Taylor leaned back on the sofa, spread her legs, and extended the invitation. Victor retrieved a condom from the pocket of his slacks, tore into the golden wrapper, and rolled it down his hard, thick shaft. He dropped to his knees and slowly guided the swollen head inside of her. She felt a sweet pain as she stretched to accommodate him. He exhaled a harsh breath as he sank deeper. Stunned by the initial invasion, Taylor forced her muscles to relax around him. He began to slowly ease in and out of her slick pussy, and Taylor found herself moving along with him. He was filling her completely. The friction of their coupling was

CREED
by *Phoenix Daniels*

igniting a spark that was sure to lead to orgasmic bliss. He pushed her knees into her chest and fucked her with aggression; so hard and so deep that he was fucking her soul. Taylor, without shame, shouted his name over and over.

Victor roughly grabbed her bouncing breast, pinching and kneading her nipples. Beads of sweat trickled down his strong torso. The sound of their bodies colliding echoed throughout the room.

"Damn, sweetheart," he grunted. "You're so fucking tight. I'm gonna fuck your tight little pussy all night; then I'm gonna lick it, and fuck you some more."

His dirty words were a direct line to her sex, taking her to the boiling point.

"Yes! Ugh! You... feel so damn good. I'm cum-ming!" she screamed, hearing the hoarseness in her own voice.

Like a volcano, she erupted so hard that she could see the proof of her violent orgasm splashing against his tight abs. Taylor howled as she came harder than she ever had in her entire life. And he was right with her. After one powerful thrust, he stilled. His dick pulsed as he pumped hot cum into the condom. Taylor could feel the warmth, even through the protective barrier.

But, if Taylor thought that he was done, she was wrong. Because, as promised, he licked and fucked her all night long.

CREED
by *Phoenix Daniels*

✳✳✳✳_✳

The incessant shrill of her ringing phone jerked Taylor from a deep sleep. She peeked over her shoulder to check the time. It was barely seven in the morning. She reached on the nightstand and grabbed her cell. It was an unknown number. She swiped to ignore and returned it to the nightstand. But no sooner than her head hit the pillow, it rang again. She snatched the phone and swiped.

"What?!" she snapped in a groggy voice.

"Miss Montgomery?"

"What?" she repeated into the phone.

"Miss Montgomery, I'm sorry to bother you, but the governor isn't answering his phone."

"Who... who is this?"

"It's Kenyatta, ma'am, Kena, Governor Creed's assistant."

"Oh," Taylor said, sitting up.

His incredibly pretty, Black assistant.

"He's asleep," Taylor groaned.

"Miss Montgomery, the governor..."

"Taylor. Call me Taylor."

CREED
by *Phoenix Daniels*

"Yes, okay, Taylor, the governor has a very important meeting at eight. Please wake him and let him know that I'll be bringing him a change of clothes in thirty minutes."

Taylor wondered if Victor ever made a move that Kenyatta wasn't aware of. She somehow doubted it.

"Um... I'll... okay."

"Thanks, Taylor."

"No problem."

Taylor rolled over. The sight of Victor sleeping on his back with one hand behind his head and the other covering his balls caused her to shiver. His rock-hard body was a total contradiction to the softness in his face as he slept. She admired his beauty as she ran her fingers over the soft hairs on his chest.

"Victor," she whispered softly.

He stirred but didn't wake.

"Victor," she repeated a little louder.

His eyes blinked open and landed on hers. "Good morning," he said with a boyish grin.

His voice was husky and oh so masculine.

"Good morning… Your assistant called. She'll be here in a few with a change of clothes."

His eyes roamed her naked breasts. His lids became hooded, and his gaze was filled with lust. When his hand cupped her

CREED
by *Phoenix Daniels*

breast, slid down her side and over her hip to grope her ass, carnal thoughts came over her as well.

"Victor," she warned. "She said you have a meeting at eight."

Sliding his body over hers, he responded, "I'm gonna be late."

CREED

by *Phoenix Daniels*

CHAPTER 7

TAYLOR

Taylor pulled in front of Roseland Beauty Supply on Michigan Avenue. Maria wanted to pick up some conditioner before it got too busy to stop. They took off their seatbelts and prepared to get out when a vehicle flew dangerously through the red light. Normally, Taylor and Maria didn't write traffic tickets, but the driver's blatant disregard for the traffic signal was dangerous. Taylor looked over at Maria, who was refastening her seatbelt, and quickly fastened her own. She pulled away from the curb and maneuvered through traffic until she was directly behind the driver. Maria ran the plates on the portable data terminal (PDT), as Taylor activated the Mars lights. When the driver didn't pull over right away, she pointed the spotlight on their side view mirror. The driver, finally getting the message, pulled to the side. Taylor pulled behind the Ford Fusion just as a report came back on the PDT. The owner of the vehicle was clear and not wanted for anything, so Taylor and Maria exited the squad car.

Taylor approached the driver's side, and Maria covered the passenger side. The driver rolled down his window with a panicked expression.

CREED
by *Phoenix Daniels*

"Sir, you totally disregarded the red light back there. I need your license and proof of insurance."

"I know. I'm sorry," the male driver said in an apologetic, but frantic tone.

"M-my wife... she's in labor!"

Taylor looked over at the passenger seat. The panting woman was indeed very pregnant. Taylor looked at Maria over the hood of the car and nodded.

"Ma'am, please step out of the car," Maria insisted.

"What?! Are you fucking serious?! No!" the man protested.

"Yes, sir," Taylor responded calmly.

"We have emergency lights, and we can get your wife to the hospital a lot faster. We'll get you there, sir."

The driver breathed a sigh of relief. "Oh, okay, thank you so much."

He hopped out of the car and helped Maria ease his wife out of the car. They walked her to the front seat of the squad car and carefully eased her inside.

"Sir, my partner is going to drive your wife to Christ Hospital, and since we'll be runnin' lights and stuff, I'm going to drive your car."

"Thank you so much, officer. Thank you soooo much," he said with a smile.

CREED
by *Phoenix Daniels*

His sincerity made Taylor smile. She hopped in the driver's seat, pulled out behind Maria, and violated every traffic law to get the man and his wife to the hospital.

A few hours later, Taylor and Maria picked up a quick lunch from Subway and headed back to Christ. Maria wanted to check up on the expecting couple. They were in the small room that cops and CFD paramedics normally occupied and enjoyed their submarines when Nancy, the ER nurse, walked in smiling.

"I called OB. They had a boy. He was 7lbs, 5 ounces."

"Thanks, Nancy," Maria responded, smiling.

"No problem. I'll see y'all later."

Nancy walked out of the room. Taylor and Maria finished their lunch and went back out on the street.

"2234," Taylor called to the dispatcher.

"Go, 2234."

"We're clear from lunch squad."

"10-4."

Taylor patrolled their beat, thankful for the momentary quiet. She immediately thought about Victor. It had been weeks since they'd spent that first night together, and they'd been joined at the hip ever since. Lying next to him at night felt like second nature to her, and on one of the few nights that they were apart, she often

CREED
by *Phoenix Daniels*

found herself unable to sleep. She was loving the hot, mind-blowing sex, followed by sweet kisses and cuddling.

They didn't have conventional dates, but they had enjoyed intimate dinners, watched movies in the theater inside of the Governor's Mansion, and taken long romantic walks on the grounds. Taylor loved conversing with him about things that most folks avoided. They had endless discussions about religion, politics, even race. She understood why the people voted him into office; he had a genuine desire to make the world a better place. He seemed to really understand the needs of the people of Illinois. That didn't mean that he wasn't a true politician, though. Victor definitely knew how to grease the wheel. Still, he was a good man who cared about people and loved his family. He often spoke of his little brothers with love and admiration. Because of that, Taylor truly admired him.

"2234?"

Taylor responded into the radio. "34, go."

"I got a traffic crash with injuries; 103rd and State Street."

"10-4. We're en route."

"10-4."

"Ugh," Maria groaned. "I hate doing traffic crash reports."

CREED
by *Phoenix Daniels*

So did Taylor, and she was happy for the first time that night that it was her turn to drive and Maria's turn to do the reports. Maria groaned again, and Taylor smiled on the inside.

CHAPTER 8
CREED

Victor stifled a yawn as Kenyatta read off his scheduled appointments.

"Maybe you should try sleeping at home sometimes," she snarled.

"Maybe you should stick to doing your job and stay out of my personal business."

"Uhh... I'm your *personal* assistant. You wouldn't survive a week without me."

"Correction, you're my executive assistant. Aaand... if I may add, your busybody ass is the exact reason why I don't have a personal assistant," Victor chuckled.

"Hmph, like I said, you wouldn't last a week without me," Kenyatta muttered under her breath.

Suddenly, Lisa's voice came through the intercom. "Governor Creed, you have a call waiting."

Kena reached over his desk and pushed the intercom. "Lisa, I asked you to hold the governor's calls until we were done going over his calendar."

"Yes, but it's Miss Montgomery."

CREED
by *Phoenix Daniels*

"Oh, ok, thank you, Lisa. Put her through," she said as she stood to her feet.

The mention of Taylor's name caused Victor to smile. They'd spent almost every night of the last three months in her bed. Victor had even found himself waiting for her when she got off late at night. His unprecedented actions surprised even him. He dreaded the night that he couldn't roll over and push inside of her. And he prayed that she didn't, one day, come home and tell him that she didn't feel like being bothered. He simply didn't see that as being an option.

The phone rang just as Kenyatta exited his office. He picked up on the first ring.

"Hello, gorgeous."

"Hey, baby, I'm sorry I missed your call. I was in roll call."

"It's fine. What time do you think you'll be home tonight?"

Fuck! Did I just say that?

"If nothing happens, I shouldn't be too late."

"I'm looking forward to this weekend."

"Yesss! Me too!"

The excitement in her voice gripped his heart. He could picture her beautiful smile in his mind.

"Baby, I gotta go hit the streets."

"All right. You be careful."

CREED

by *Phoenix Daniels*

"Yes, governor."

"Baby, you know your obedience makes my cock hard. Don't tease me."

She giggled devilishly.

"Ok, baby, later."

"Later."

Before Victor could return the receiver, Kenyatta's voice reminded him that he had a budget meeting in ten minutes.

"Thanks, Kenyatta. Anything from Kara Edwards?"

"Not a peep. But, of course, she will be present during your press conference."

"Whoopee," Victor said with absolutely no enthusiasm. "Grab Lisa and be ready in five."

"Aye aye, sir."

CREED

by *Phoenix Daniels*

TAYLOR

Since it was Maria's turn to drive, Taylor leaned against the wall and waited as she signed out radios from the equipment room.

"You two bitches betta not go out there and kick off no shit tonight," sniggered Robert Hills. He was the joke telling, shit talking, wisecracking, no filter having, but harmless comedian on their shift. Robert was sure to make the night interesting.

"If we don't kick shit off…," Maria chimed. "…your lazy ass wouldn't have shit to do all night."

A few officers laughed and directed jokes toward each other as they made their way out of the district. Maria glanced at the number on the keys and looked around the parking lot for the squad car with the number that matched.

"Over here," she told Taylor.

They did a quick inspection of the outside, then the inside of the vehicle before hopping in.

"Eww, who had this car last? It smells like onions and shit. No, it smells like someone has been shitting onions," Maria complained.

CREED
by *Phoenix Daniels*

She reached between the seat and pulled the trash left by the watch before. With her face twisted in disgust, she flung the trash out the window.

"Maria!" Taylor admonished.

"What? The city pays people to clean this up, don't they? You want them to lose their jobs?"

Taylor shook her head. Maria was a mess. But for Taylor, there was no other partner for her. They knew each other so well that they were damn near reading each other's minds. Maria was smart and tough, and Taylor trusted her with her life.

Maria backed out of the parking space and sped through the lot. She turned to Taylor and asked, "Who's the guy?"

"What guy?" Taylor asked, feigning ignorance.

She knew exactly what guy Maria meant, however.

"If I have to ask you again, I'm gonna crash this motherfuckin' car and kill us both."

Taylor laughed. "Okay, I am seeing someone."

"For a few months now," Maria added.

"Now, how would you know that?"

"Girl, I spend more time with you than anyone else in my life; at least, ten hours a day. I know everything about you."

She was right, and she knew just about everything about Maria. She could gauge her mood better than her husband could.

CREED
by *Phoenix Daniels*

"Spill. Who's the guy? And please tell me he's not a cop."

"He's an amazingly sweet, sexy, and considerate man. And, no, he's not a cop."

"Well, who is he?"

"His name is Victor, Victor Creed."

"Hmm... like the governor," Maria mused.

"Yes, just like the governor."

Maria drove in silence for about fifteen seconds before pulling over. She put the car in park, turned to face Taylor, and asked, "Taylor, are you seeing *Governor* Victor Creed?"

"Yes, I'm dating the governor. Can you please keep it to yourself?"

"Get the fuck out! You're dating the governor of Illinois?"

Taylor nodded.

"Is it just a hookup or you're really *seeing* each other?"

"I'll just say this, and then you can decide for yourself; we've slept next to each other almost every night for the last few months. Well, we eventually get to sleep," Taylor said with a chuckle.

"Adios mios."

"Maria, promise me that you won't tell anyone."

"Girl, your secret is safe with me. I gotta tell ya, though; that motherfucka is fine! Wooh!"

CREED
by *Phoenix Daniels*

"That he is," Taylor agreed.

Maria fanned herself before shifting into drive. She pulled out in traffic and began to patrol their South Side beat. All seemed to be quiet. Well, quiet for the South Side anyway. But they patrolled none the less. Even the radio was quiet. But since it was bad luck to comment on the silence of the radio, neither one them spoke of it out loud. Taylor was just grateful for a peaceful night. A peaceful night ensured that she would get home at a reasonable hour so that she could be with Victor.

Her thoughts wandered to the conversation that they'd had that morning. He wanted to know if she would be okay if their relationship became public. The topic was a bit of a surprise to Taylor. She somehow thought that he preferred to keep their thing private. After all, he was the governor. She was very pleasantly surprised that he was fine with the world knowing that he wanted her. The conversation was a total contradiction to the one she had with her sister.

"Girl, he's just slumming in your pussy," is what Nicole had told her. *"You gonna be his dirty little secret."*

But what Nicole didn't know was that Taylor preferred to keep their relationship private. She had planned to advance in the department, and she didn't want to hear any rumors about her success being attributed to her fucking the governor.

CREED
by *Phoenix Daniels*

"Heads up," Maria warned, diverting Taylor's attention.

She quickly scanned the area, soon realizing what Maria was referring to. A white Lexus was waiting at a traffic light directly in front of them. The right turn signal was blinking at a rapid pace, but the Lexus was in the left turning lane. Now to most, it would have been no big deal. But to Taylor and Maria, it meant a little more. Maria turned left with the Lexus and waited for the driver to turn off the turn signal. But once the turn was made, the driver made another left. The right turn signal was still active. A jammed turned signal is the first clue that a vehicle was stolen. Taylor reached for the radio clipped to her shoulder.

"2234," she announced.

"2234, go ahead," the dispatcher responded.

"Squad, please run a plate."

"Go with your plate."

"T, as in Tom, 392308, on a white Lexus, Squad."

"10-4. What's your location, 2234?"

"Westbound on 115th, coming up on Racine."

"10-4, 2234. Standby."

Maria followed the Lexus at a moderate speed as they waited for the dispatcher to get back to them.

"2234?"

"34, go."

CREED
by *Phoenix Daniels*

"Your vehicle is coming back stolen from-"

Before the dispatcher could finish, the driver of the Lexus slammed on the brakes. The driver's door flew open, and the driver took off on foot. Maria looked over at Taylor expectantly. Of course, they would get into a foot chase when it was Maria's turn to drive. Taylor rolled her eyes and bowed out of the vehicle in pursuit.

The chase began.

Taylor could hear her partner on the radio.

"2234! Emergency!

"Units standby," the dispatcher announced.

"2234, you have the air. Where are you?"

"Alley...Southbound... Squad... From 115th," Taylor huffed and puffed, trying to run and speak into the radio at the same time.

"Alley... East... of ... Ashland"

"Who ya chasin'?" the dispatcher asked.

"Male, Black, or maybe, Hispanic, white t-shirt, blue jeans!" Taylor shouted into the radio.

Taylor ran hard behind the fleeing offender, but she was losing ground. She pushed as hard as she could just to keep him in sight. She could hear the dispatcher announcing her foot chase and calling for backup. She had also heard other officers

CREED
by *Phoenix Daniels*

announce over the air that they were en route to provide backup. She heard tires screeching from several angles, so she knew that help was close.

The distance between her and the driver was getting wider, however, and Taylor was getting winded. None the less, she kept pushing. Just when she was ready to call it, another squad car cut the runner off. The driver, Jim Gore, and his partner, Trevor, jumped out of the vehicle with their weapons drawn. Relief flooded through Taylor as her exhaustion kicked in. She stopped running in order to catch a much-needed breath. She turned to the sound of tires on gravel. It was Maria. She knew that she was close by. She slapped the hood of the squad car and pointed to the end of the alley, where her offender was standing with his hands on his head, pacing back and forward, and gulping as much oxygen as he could. He was, seemingly as out of breath as Taylor. Only when Taylor was twenty-five feet away from her prisoner and was satisfied that he was about to be taken into custody, did she truly relax. But as she approached, the sound of a shot being fired caused her to instinctively snatch her weapon from its holster. She looked at her offender, but his hands were still on his head, fingers interlocked. She looked for the source of the noise. It was then that she realized that it was her backup, Gore that had

CREED
by *Phoenix Daniels*

fired the shot. He'd shot her offender, who was unarmed. He stood still a few seconds before collapsing to the ground.

"Oh, fuck me!" she heard Maria shout from behind.

CREED
by *Phoenix Daniels*

CHAPTER 9
TAYLOR

Taylor and Maria leaned against their squad car, staying out of the way. The scene had become chaotic. Crime scene tape separated the police personnel from cell phone wielding civilians. In a matter of minutes, the once quiet alley was filled with activity. There were a number of supervisors, crime scene technicians, paramedics, nosey police officers, and more importantly, the corpse of a man who, less than thirty minutes ago, was alive and standing with his hands behind his head.

"Taylor, what did you see?" Maria asked in a whisper.

"I saw the same gotdamn thing that you saw."

"Ugh... This is fucked up," Maria muttered.

Taylor sighed. "Yeah, it's pretty fucked up."

Although Taylor had avoided all eye contact with Jim, she could physically feel the burn of his stare. He was having an animated conversation with the watch commander, no doubt trying to explain why he'd just shot an unarmed man. Taylor looked over at the growing crowd and wondered why the body hadn't been removed yet. It was the true center of a spectacle.

"She was the one chasing them," one accuser voiced.

CREED

by *Phoenix Daniels*

"These motherfuckas gun'n us down every chance they get!" shouted another.

"Oh shit. Here they come," Maria grumbled.

Taylor looked up to see the watch commander, the street lieutenant, and the sector sergeant walking her way, with Gore following close behind.

And so it begins.

Taylor pushed off the car, but Maria maintained her relaxed position.

The watch commander spoke first. "Mendez, Montgomery, we need you two to go in and give your statements and fill out supplementary reports."

"Okay," Maria said, standing straight, ready to get in the car.

"Just so you know before you go…," the watch commander said, slowing her progress. "Officer Gore and his partner stated that they came in contact with the offender when they were assisting you in your foot chase. He charged at them, causing them to fear for their safety, and that's when Officer Gore fired at him."

"Is that what they say?" Taylor asked as she turned her suspicious gaze to Jim Gore.

"Yeah," he responded with narrowed eyes.

"Bullshit," Maria hissed.

CREED
by *Phoenix Daniels*

"Bullshit?" The Lieutenant questioned.

"Yes, bullshit," Taylor confirmed. "That's not what happened here, and I ain't cosigning that shit."

"Me either," Maria chimed.

"Bitch!" Gore lashed, through gritted teeth. "You better get on board."

"You want me to get on board with you shootin' folks in cold blood? Mmm umph!" Taylor said, shaking her head. "I'll pass on that."

With that being said, the battle ensued. All present began to bicker back and forth. But when their voices began to amplify beyond their closed circle, the watch commander shut it down and ordered everyone into the station. Gore and his partner shot threatening glares at Taylor and Maria before walking away. Taylor turned and walked toward the passenger side.

"Taylor! Taylor Montgomery!" She heard coming from the crowd of onlookers on the other side of the police tape.

Taylor searched the crowd for the source. It was Brent Trainer, the reporter that Taylor had to knock on his ass a little while ago.

"Taylor, can you give me a statement?!" he shouted.

"Yeah, you're a jagoff that can't keep his hands to himself!" Taylor shouted in return, before getting in the car.

CREED
by *Phoenix Daniels*

"So, that's the prince that Nic set you up with, huh?" Maria asked.

"The one and only."

"Tay, there are news cameras everywhere. This is gonna be a huge mess," Maria sighed.

"Yeah, I know. And we're right in the middle of it. Sadly, we only have two choices. One, we could protect our fellow officer and back his statement, essentially condoning murder. Or, two, we could give an honest statement and risk being ostracized by the department and the very officers that we depend on for backup. It'll be fucked up either way," Taylor explained. "At any rate, my choice has been made."

CREED

by *Phoenix Daniels*

CREED

Victor sat behind the desk in his home office and worried. He'd been to Taylor's house, and she wasn't there. She wasn't answering her phone either. It was 2am, and she was supposed to be off at midnight. With Taylor being a police officer, it was easy to fear the worst. For that reason, he'd charged Collier with finding her.

No longer able to stare at the wall opposite of him, he grabbed the remote control and turned on the television. He surfed the channels in search of the world news. It was then that he saw the very woman that he was looking for. The reporter stated the she was on the scene of a shooting that occurred on the South Side. It was clear that Taylor wasn't hurt, but she seemed to be in the middle of a heated argument with some other officers.

A knock at the door diverted his attention from the television. "Come in."

"Sir, Miss Montgomery is at the 22nd police district. There was an incident on-"

"Yes, Collier, I gathered that. Get the car."

"But, sir, I have to alert your security detail."

"Then alert them."

CREED

by *Phoenix Daniels*

Victor grabbed his suit coat from the back of his chair. Whether she needed him or not, he was on his way to the 22nd district.

CHAPTER 10
TAYLOR

Taylor handed Captain Hale, the watch commander, her supplementary report, containing her eyewitness account of the shooting and everything that led to it. He scanned her report and looked up at her over his reading glasses. His pale, wrinkled face was masked with disappointment.

"So, this is the route you're taking?"

Taylor's response was laced with determination. "It's what happened."

"With the climate of police/citizen relations, I shouldn't have to tell you that we don't need this right now."

"What's your point, Captain? Do you want me to lie about what I saw?"

The captain jumped to his feet and closed in on Taylor, so close that she could smell coffee and stale cigarettes on his breath.

"Watch yourself, Montgomery. I am not the one to fuck with," he roared. "Now get your self-righteous ass out of my office!"

Taylor, without flinching, stood her ground. "Who do you think you're talking to? With all due respect, I'm an adult, and

CREED
by *Phoenix Daniels*

that is not how you speak to adults. Now, you watch how the hell you speak to me," she responded with a calm that only seemed to piss him off more.

"Officer Montgomery..." he began, but his retaliation was cut off.

"Is there a problem here?"

The authoritative voice of the governor silenced the room. Taylor slowly turned to face Victor. She was shocked by his presence, but not half as shocked as Captain Hale. He'd turned white as a sheet.

"Gov... n-no, Gov... Creed... sir," he stammered nervously. "It's fine, sir; just police business."

"I'd like a minute," Victor ordered.

"Yes, sir. Montgomery, you're dismissed."

Taylor narrowed her eyes at the weaselly little man and turned to leave the room. As she walked past Victor, she closed her eyes and discreetly inhaled the enticing aroma of all man. She walked across the station to the stairs that led to the locker room, where she was joined by Maria.

"What is your boyfriend doing here?" Maria whispered.

"Boyfriend?"

"Yeah, what's he doing here?"

CREED
by *Phoenix Daniels*

"Well, if I were to guess by all the cameras, I would assume that he heard about the shooting. He's probably trying to prevent a riot from breaking out."

"Did he speak? Hug you? Kiss you? What?" Maria asked as they entered the locker room.

"Of course not. Are you nuts? He just said that he needed to talk to Hale."

"You didn't feel weird?"

"Why would I feel weird? No one knows about us."

"Shit, Taylor, that man is beautiful, way more beautiful than you by the way."

"Maria, you can go straight to hell," Taylor joked.

"Wait," Maria said, looking around in feigned shock. "This ain't hell?"

Taylor chuckled. "It's about to be,"

CREED

Victor listened to the captain stutter through the night's incident as long as he could before he asked, "Why were you speaking to that officer with such disrespect?"

The captain was completely thrown off by the change of subject. "Who? Montgomery? She's a pain in my ass; downright insubordinate. She refuses to go along with the program."

"What's the program, Captain Hale?"

"I'm trying to prevent a major incident here. With all this Black Lives Matter shit, a shooting like this could incite a riot. She just won't listen to reason."

"You mean you want her to lie."

"That's not what I said, Governor Creed. I'm just saying-"

"You were just saying that Officer Montgomery won't lie, at your behest, about what she witnessed."

"She's probably lying about what she saw. She's a disgruntled, militant, feminist. If you ask me, the worst thing this city could have done was allow women in the police department."

Victor closed the distance between them and stared down at the shorter man. The captain tensed and clutched the edge of his desk.

CREED
by *Phoenix Daniels*

"I didn't ask you. And it would behoove you to watch what you say about Taylor Montgomery. Your life depends on it, you piece of shit. And if I ever hear about you disrespecting or trash talking Taylor, I'm coming back for your ass."

As Victor turned to leave the office, he heard Hale ask, "Governor Creed, sir, who is Officer Montgomery to you?"

"None of your fucking business," he answered as he left the office.

CREED

by *Phoenix Daniels*

TAYLOR

After changing out of their uniforms, Taylor and Maria left the locker room and headed down the stairs. They walked over to the district desk, avoiding Gore and Trevor, his dumb, rookie partner. Gore was attempting to intimidate them with his best version of a threatening glare. Had the situation not been so serious, she would have laughed in his face.

"Can I have a time slip?" she asked the desk sergeant.

It was 3:30 am, and she was working on overtime. Taylor's night had been thoroughly fucked up, and she'd be damn if she didn't get paid for it.

Just as the sergeant handed her and Maria overtime slips, Victor was walking out of the watch commander's office, with Captain Hale on his heel like a puppy. He was practically running behind Victor, until Gregor placed his big body in his path. The watch commander hadn't expected to run into the equivalent of a wall. Taylor couldn't help the giggle that escaped when he bounced off of Gregor, lost his footing, and fell on his rear end. Seeing her supervisor fall was funny, but her laughter ceased when she saw that Victor was walking in her direction. Her eyes widened in an effort to send a message to him to go in the other

CREED
by *Phoenix Daniels*

direction. Apparently, Victor couldn't read eye language, because he walked right up to her and slipped his arm around her waist.

"It's late. Leave your car. You're coming home with me tonight," he said in a sexy, authoritative tone that left no room for refusal.

Taylor looked around, and every eye in the station was fixed on her.

"Okay!" Maria volunteered, forcing a nervous chuckle from Taylor.

Victor turned to Maria and extended his hand with a smile. "Maria, right? I've heard a great deal about you. It's nice to finally meet you."

"All good I'm sure," Maria said as she shook Victor's hand.

"Nope, sorry," he jested, causing her to narrow her eyes at Taylor.

Taylor fidgeted with her hands while they exchanged pleasantries. Neither of them was not at all that concerned that Victor had just outed their relationship.

"Okay, bye, Maria. Victor, let's go," Taylor urged.

She walked over to Gregor, hoping it would hurry Victor along.

"Wow," she mumbled under her breath.

CREED
by *Phoenix Daniels*

"Wow is right," Gregor mumbled in return. "I've yet to witness a public display of affection on the governor's part."

Gregor's words hit Taylor like a brick. It wasn't the first time that Victor's actions implied that their relationship was more than casual, but they'd never had the discussion. The most they discussed was whether or not Taylor was willing to date him in the open. Obviously, he'd made the decision for her, unless he was truly unaware of how fast gossip traveled through the police department. Victor wasn't a naive man, so she somehow doubted that. Still, Taylor had no plans to initiate the conversation. Although she wanted Victor more than she cared to admit, she didn't want to scare the man away. She cared for him, and she was having such a wonderful time with him, but she had no way of knowing what was really in his head. So, Taylor planned to ride the hell out of that wave before the ocean dried up.

CREED
by *Phoenix Daniels*

CHAPTER 11
TAYLOR

Taylor and Victor followed Gregor into Victor's apartment. It was the first time she'd entered his apartment since their first date. And to Taylor's surprise, Gregor hadn't confiscated her weapon.

She walked across the foyer, into the living room, and flopped down on the sofa.

"Don't get too comfortable," Victor said. "I'm gonna go run you a bath."

Running her a bath was something that he often did for her whenever he'd spend the night at her house. She'd wash away all remnants of her hectic night with the help of candles and soft music.

"Thank you, baby," she said to his back as he walked out of the room.

She rested her head against the back of the sofa and thought of their conversation during the ride to his place. She'd told herself that she wouldn't bring up the topic of their relationship, but Taylor just couldn't help herself.

"Victor, why did you do that?"

"Do what?"

CREED
by *Phoenix Daniels*

"You know exactly what you did. You just let every cop in the station know that we're sleeping together. That shit's gonna be all over the police department by tomorrow."

"So? You ashamed of me? I mean really; I'm the governor of Illinois for God's sake. You could do a lot worse than me," he chortled.

"Victor, this ain't no joke. I'm already the main topic of conversation in the station."

"I'm sorry, Taylor, but we're an item. You're not gonna be able to hide that forever. Now, we're both consenting adults, and we're doing nothing wrong. I don't want a secret affair. I want everyone to know that this is my pussy."

"Nice," Taylor said shaking her head.

"Yeah, put your big girl panties on and date the governor."

"Ugh, I'm never gonna get promoted."

Victor looked at her and laughed. "Don't worry, sweetheart. After blatantly refusing to back up that bullshit story, you were definitely not running the risk of being promoted."

"That's not funny, Victor," Taylor said with a pout.

Sadly, the more Taylor thought about their conversation, the more she realized that Victor might have been right. Grudges lasted a long time in the department. She squeezed her eyes

CREED
by *Phoenix Daniels*

closed and tried to not to think of the proverbial nail in the proverbial coffin that housed her career.

"Come, sweetness. Your bath is ready."

Victor's deep masculine voice echoed through the apartment. She opened her eyes to the sight of his well-formed, shirtless chest. His thick dark hair had fallen in his beautifully sculpted face, and his green eyes were sparkling like stars.

"Victor, you're gorgeous. You know that?"

"Gorgeous? Well, as long as you think so, I'm happy. But gorgeous is a description that best suits you, sweetness. Come on," he said, holding out his hand. "Let me bathe you."

"Yes, dear," Taylor murmured as she lifted her tired body off of the couch.

✳✳✳✳

Taylor lowered herself into the luxurious tub that made hers seem like a crock-pot. She looked around and determined that her entire bedroom could fit in Victor's bathroom. She slid further into the water and inhaled the fresh scent of candles and bubble bath while allowing the warmth of the water to ease the tension in her tight muscles.

"I'm never leaving this tub," Taylor moaned.

CREED
by *Phoenix Daniels*

"That's too bad because I got something out here waiting for you," he responded, donning a wicked grin, and grabbing his package.

"You might just have to bring that in here with me."

Taylor seductively drew slow circles around her wet nipple, before allowing her fingers to glide down her body and disappear into the water. Her provocative actions sparked her own arousal. She gasped softly as her fingers connected with her swollen clit. A moan escaped her parted lips as she manipulated the swollen nerve-filled bud. Victor massaged his visibly hard dick over his slacks as he watched Taylor pleasure herself.

"Let me see you cum, sweetness."

His deep lustful voice rumbled her insides, causing her to tremble. Victor unbuckled his belt, and Taylor became excited for what was to come. But the sound of his ringing phone and the knock at his bedroom door were like nails on a chalkboard.

"Gotdamnit!" he cursed loudly. "Don't move. I'll be right back."

He hurried out of the bathroom. Taylor could hear his heavy footsteps as he stomped across his bedroom. She heard muffled voices before the bedroom door was slammed. For what seemed like forever, she sat patiently in the tub until the water began to cool.

CREED
by *Phoenix Daniels*

I guess playtime is over, she thought to herself as she stepped out of the bathtub onto a plush bath mat.

Taylor grabbed a towel and patted her skin before wrapping the towel around her body. She exited the bathroom and entered Victor's colossal bedroom. She searched his dresser drawers until she found one of his t-shirts. Taylor quickly threw it over her head and walked out of his bedroom.

"Who the fuck is she?!" she heard coming from the loud, angry voice of a woman.

Taylor stopped in her tracks, deciding to let Victor handle the irate woman on his own. She'd been yelled at enough tonight. Not to mention, enough people knew more than they should about her personal life. She'd allow Victor to explain the intrusion later. For now, all she wanted was sleep. She would deal with her job and Victor's issues later.

She walked back into the bedroom and slid under the cool sheets. Taylor was physically and emotionally exhausted. And no sooner than she heard Victor's front door slam, she closed her heavy lids and found herself in Lala Land.

****

CREED
by *Phoenix Daniels*

Warmth encased Taylor's center. The overwhelming feeling of elation caused her to squirm. Her own moan woke her from a deep slumber. Even before her lids fluttered open, she knew what was happening. Victor was bringing her to ecstasy with his mouth; licking, sucking, and flicking his tongue over her already wet pussy.

"Ohh, Victor," she groaned. "Yessss, baby."

Although it seemed as if she'd just closed her eyes, the sun had come up. She was still so tired, but that didn't matter, because he was making her feel so good, taking her to a place where she could give less than a damn about the time that had lapsed. She just wanted more.

"Ummm."

His tongue was a lesson in the best torture. The pure unadulterated pleasure of it was almost too much to bear. But stopping him was not an option. It was so good; so good in fact that Taylor was already nearing an impending orgasm. She gripped a good portion of his thick, beautiful hair and fucked his face without mercy.

"Victor!" she shouted, thrashing her head from side to side. "Ima come, baby. Ima come so hard!"

Taylor could hear the groan of approval deep in his throat. It was just the incentive needed for her to implode.

CREED
by *Phoenix Daniels*

"Aghh!!! My Go-o---d!!! Yessss!" she shouted as her body convulsed violently. But before she could ride the last wave of her orgasm, he pushed himself, large and unbelievably hard, into her and proceeded to fuck her senseless.

Three orgasms later, she was asleep again.

CHAPTER 12
CREED

Victor rested his head under the warm stream of the shower. He'd only had a few hours of sleep. He'd still be in the bed had it not been for Taylor's energetic ass. She'd awakened him with a mind-blowing blowjob, before announcing that she was going to the kitchen to prepare breakfast. The woman was a ball of fire that he thought he'd doused in the night. But, apparently, her flame wouldn't be easily put out.

It was 7am, and they had plans to go fishing with Taylor's dad. Victor was taking them to his lake house in southern Illinois. He had bragged to James about the abundance of Bluegills. Victor knew that he was dragging. And although he had set the date and time for their excursion, he hadn't accounted for the unforeseen shooting the night before.

Victor quickly finished his shower, dressed, and made his way to the kitchen. He found Taylor standing in front of the stove with her hair bouncing wild and free down her back. She was, to him, the most beautiful woman that he'd ever seen. She was wearing one of his t-shirts, and her full hips were swaying to the reggae music that was blaring through the speakers. He wanted to bend her over the stove and beast fuck her from behind, but he

CREED
by *Phoenix Daniels*

just stood there and watched, enjoying the sight of her. He wanted her so badly. If she wasn't his already, it was his goal to make her his as soon as possible. His plan was to sign his name all over her pussy and solidify his position in her life.

"Who was the angry woman that was shoutin' at the top of her lungs in your living room last night?" she asked without turning around.

Here we go.

"How did you know I was behind you?" Victor asked.

"I can smell you. You smell like fine ass man."

Victor smiled, loving the compliment. "Fine ass man, huh?"

"The woman?" she repeated, not allowing him to change the subject.

Victor walked over to her, grabbed a fistful of her curly hair and gently yanked her head back, giving him access to her lips.

"Good morning, sweetness," he whispered, just before kissing her lips.

"Good morning, baby," she mumbled against his lips. "I made coffee."

"Thanks."

He swatted her ass, walked over to the cabinet, and grabbed a cup. "Her name's Kara, Kara Edwards. She's my press

CREED

by *Phoenix Daniels*

secretary," he explained as he poured coffee into his cup. "Do you want a cup?"

She raised her cup to show that she'd already had coffee. "What's the deal with Miss Kara Edwards, Victor?"

Clearly, Taylor wasn't accepting the vague explanation. Maybe if she got tired of being a cop, there was a job for her as a reporter.

Wait, Victor thought. *Cops interrogate people too.*

He almost laughed out loud at the banter going on in his head, until Taylor turned around and stared pointedly at him.

"We had a thing," he finally answered.

"A thing?"

"Yeah, we were sleeping together," Victor admitted. "Recently. But we ended it."

"We? It didn't sound like shit had ended for her."

"Yeah," was all he said.

"'Sleeping together' was that the extent of your relationship?"

"Yes, sweetness. We had that understanding."

"Maybe you had that understanding, but I guarantee you that she didn't have that understanding."

"Doesn't matter," Victor responded in a tone that was matter of fact.

CREED
by *Phoenix Daniels*

Taylor carried a skillet containing an omelet to the table and slid the eggs onto Victor's plate. Victor took a seat in front of the plate and looked down at the perfect omelet.

He smiled up at Taylor. "I love it when you cook for me."

"Then I gotta cook for you more often," she said, leaning over to give him a sweet kiss.

With Victor's eyes fixed on her luscious ass, she walked across the kitchen to place the skillet in the sink. He'd never seen an ass so perfect. When Taylor turned toward him, stealing away his perfect view, he simply focused on her big braless tits. She was a vision. Suddenly, it came to him; he was going to commission an artist to paint her.

"She's going to be trouble," Taylor said, diverting his attention.

"She won't, sweetheart. Let me worry about Kara Edwards. You worry about enjoying your breakfast. Come and sit."

Taylor did as instructed. She sat in the chair next to him and forked a big chunk of eggs. But before the fork made it into her mouth, Kenyatta burst into the kitchen with a horrified look on her face.

Victor cringed. *What now?*

"Sir, you have seen this?" she asked, placing a newspaper in front of him.

CREED
by *Phoenix Daniels*

Victor, who was in mid-sip, choked on his coffee and ended up spitting it on the paper.

"What the fuck?!"

Taylor leaned over to look at the paper. Victor wanted to shield her from it, but he knew that she would she see it sooner or later. She focused on the paper and gasped loudly, before covering her mouth with her hand. She was staring at the headline, which was over pictures of the two of them; one in the police station with his arm around her waist and the other of them entering his building hand in hand. The headline was in big bold letters that read: **GOVERNOR SPOTTED WITH MARRIED LOVER.**

Taylor's dark skin turned almost pale. She looked as if she was going to faint at any moment.

CHAPTER 13
TAYLOR

Surely, she hadn't seen what she thought she saw. It was all a nightmare, and she would wake up soon. She heard Victor and Kenyatta's muffled voices, but couldn't focus on what they were saying. She was wheezing, battling to catch her breath. When Victor placed a paper bag to her face, she realized that she was hyperventilating. She took slow deep breaths in the paper bag until her breathing returned to normal. She was on the front page of a major newspaper, as the governor's married lover no less!

"Taylor," Victor called. "Taylor, are you okay?"

"I'm fine," she muttered breathlessly.

Kenyatta's tone was business-like as she asked, "Miss Montgomery, are you married?"

"No, I'm divorced. I've been divorced for six years."

"Legally?" she asked for clarification.

"Yes, legally. Surely you had me checked out when I started spending time with Victor."

Kenyatta didn't deny it. In fact, she nodded in agreement.

"Then why did you ask?" Taylor asked.

"Just wanted verbal confirmation."

CREED
by *Phoenix Daniels*

Taylor snatched the paper and stared at it. The photo that was taken at the station had to have been taken by an officer, but she had no clue who took the photo outside of Victor's building. She couldn't believe that her private life had been plastered across the Sun-Times. Between the shooting and the media, her life was suddenly spinning out of control.

"I'll take care of this," Victor assured, seemingly reading Taylor's mind. "I promise. Just let me handle it."

"Okay," she said in a small voice.

What else was she to say? It's not like she had an alternative. There wasn't shit that she could do. She stood on shaky legs and tossed the paper on the table.

"Look, I'm gonna go. I don't feel like fishing today. I just wanna go home."

Victor's grim expression saddened her, but she wanted to be alone, in the sanctity of her own home. She left the kitchen and headed to Victor's bedroom to get dressed. Victor hurried behind her and wrapped his arms around her waist. He snuggled his face into the crook of her neck. His warm breath tickled her skin, making her want to turn into his arms.

He held her tight and whispered, "Don't run, baby. I can fix this. I can make it right. Just don't run from me."

CREED
by *Phoenix Daniels*

She exhaled and melted into his body. "I'm not running. I'm just going home to refuel."

"Well, I hope that your tank is full by tonight because I'm coming over."

"Okay," she whispered.

Even though she wanted to be alone, she relented. Victor released a breath, seemingly relieved that she hadn't refused him.

As if she ever could.

CREED

After walking Taylor out, Victor went into the kitchen. Kenyatta was sitting at the table drinking Taylor's coffee. He grabbed the paper from the table and looked at the name under the article. It was that bastard, Brent Trainer.

"Get Kara on the phone. Tell her to get over here now. No, wait; tell her to meet me at the Thompson Center office. And get me someone that can spin this shit."

"Yes, sir."

Kenyatta finished what was left of Taylor's coffee and left the kitchen.

CREED
by *Phoenix Daniels*

TAYLOR

Taylor exited the elevator behind Gregor and followed him through the lobby. Since it was Saturday morning, the lobby wasn't as busy as it would've been on a weekday. Taylor couldn't be more grateful. She wasn't ready to face a bunch of people that could very well be judging her based on a headline that wasn't true.

A headline on the front page!

Taylor still couldn't believe that her picture was on the front page of the newspaper, and a very clear picture at that. There was no way that she'd be able to use Eddie Murphy's famous phrase, "It wasn't me." How was she going to explain that fucking article to her parents?

And, oh, God... work.

How on earth was she gonna show her face?

Taylor took a deep breath and exhaled slowly. She needed to calm down. She hoped it wouldn't be as bad as she thought. She hoped that maybe she was overreacting.

It was just one paper. Once the story dies, they will move on to something else. After all, we're in Chicago. There's always news. Hell, folks are getting whacked in the hood every day.

CREED

by *Phoenix Daniels*

Who was she kidding? There had been an actual police shooting. A man had died. That shit didn't even make the paper, and she had!

"Taylor, listen," Gregor said, halting her steps. "Collier is waiting out front. When we get out there, I want you to stay close to me, look straight ahead, and do not comment."

Taylor's heart slammed against her chest. She blinked up at Gregor in shock.

"Wait. W-what do you... What are you talking about?"

"The press."

Taylor's breath hitched. "There's press out there?"

Gregor gave Taylor a look that indicated just how stupid he thought her question was. And thus, he didn't even bother to answer. He wrapped a protective arm around her and led her out of the front door. Getting through the circus that was waiting for her was quite the feat. And judging by the amount of camera flashes and microphones shoved in her face, it was safe to say that the press wouldn't be moving on anytime soon.

Collier held the door open, donning a sympathetic expression. Gregor ushered Taylor into the back seat and slammed the door shut, but that didn't stop the cameras from flashing outside of the car. They all wanted a good shot of the governor's "married lover." Collier walked around to the driver's seat, and Gregor slid in next her.

"You did good. Now I need you to do the exact same thing when we get to your house."

"My house? Fuck!" Taylor shrieked. "Of course, they're at my house!" Taylor covered her face and slouched down in her seat.

"Miss Montgomery, please believe that the governor will handle the situation. He knows how to deal with the media," Gregor assured.

"But I don't!" Taylor snapped.

Taylor felt immediate remorse. Gregor was only trying to reassure her. He didn't deserve for her to be so short with him. "I'm sorry, Gregor. I didn't mean to-"

"It's fine. I understand, Miss Montgomery. Really, I do."

"Thanks for getting me out of there."

"You're welcome, but we're not done yet. I need the keys to your house."

Taylor nodded and fished through her purse. She handed over her keys to Gregor, who handed them over to Collier.

"Here's the plan; we're going to pull into your driveway. Collier will open your front door while we wait in the car. Once the door is open, you do it just like you did it at the tower. Okay?"

CREED
by *Phoenix Daniels*

"Okay," Taylor agreed.

But everything wasn't okay, and Taylor knew it.

CHAPTER 14

CREED

Victor didn't think that he could become more inflamed than he already was. But when Kara sashayed into his office wearing a tasteless, skin-tight dress, with a smug, satisfied look on her face, he was even more pissed. Had she been a man, he would've beat that smug look off of her face. Victor realized that he should have let her go after her fake suicide attempt. But foolishly, he thought that she would behave like an adult and eventually get over their brief fling. He was clearly wrong.

She reached for the back of the chair that sat in front of his desk.

"Don't sit," he said abruptly.

"What is it, Victor?" she asked in a bored tone.

Victor tossed the newspaper across his desk. "What the fuck is this?"

She shot a nonchalant glance at the paper and smiled. She actually fucking smiled. "Well, Governor Creed, I would say that that's a very nice picture of you and your new whore."

Victor leaned back in his chair and studied his press secretary. He wanted to leap from his seat and toss her petty ass out of the window. Victor was pissed, but he refused to give her the satisfaction of drawing any kind of emotion out of him.

"You're amused?" Victor chuckled. "Do you want me so bad that you'd allow something like this to get past you? I mean, really, Kara? Do you feel jilted or rejected enough to throw away a career that you fucked so hard to get?"

She gasped at Victor's harsh words, but he wasn't done.

"Kara, I didn't get this far by being stupid. Do you think for one goddamned minute that I didn't know that you leaked that fucking story?"

"How dare you!"

"Please save the feigned outrage. You and I both know that you have a key to the front door of the Sun-Times building. The only way that story could've gotten past you is if you planted it yourself."

"I didn't leak a damn thing!" she shouted. "You're not gonna put this shit on me."

"Why did you show up at my apartment last night, Kara? You were demanding to know who was inside; why? And, just how did you know that I had a woman inside?"

"I-I..." she stuttered.

"I'll wait," Victor said, rubbing his chin.

CREED
by *Phoenix Daniels*

Before she could fabricate an answer, Kenyatta's voice interrupted via intercom. "Governor Creed, Renee Griffin has arrived."

All the color drained from Kara's face at the mention of her biggest rival.

"You keep thinking of an answer," he said to Kara as he stood to his feet.

Renee entered Victor's office with a smile on her face; a smile that immediately disappeared when she saw Kara.

"Governor Creed, it's good to see you," she said to Victor, extending her hand.

Victor took her smaller hand in his and smiled. "Renee, thank you for coming."

"What can I do for you?" she asked, totally ignoring Kara's presence.

Victor retrieved the newspaper from his desk and handed it to her. "Can you fix this?"

"Yes, sir," she responded without even looking at the article. She'd obviously read it already.

"Hold on! What is this?!" Kara screeched.

"*This*..." Victor said, waving between Renee and himself."...is you're fired."

"Fired?!"

CREED
by *Phoenix Daniels*

"Fired," he confirmed. "Get the fuck out of my office."

"Victor, I swear to God, I will sue the pants off of you!" she screamed. "I'll tell the world that you fired me after you were done using me up. I'll let everyone know how you fucked me every chance you got and then threw me away!"

"I'll deny ever having a sexual relationship with you and paint you as the deranged, jealous, stalker that you really are," he responded with a calm that pissed her off even more.

"You're a liar!"

"No, I'm a politician," Victor chuckled. "Get the fuck out."

Kara stormed out of his office, slamming the door hard enough that it made the room shake.

Victor looked, apologetically, at Renee.

"Look, Governor Creed, if you're driving the women that crazy, please don't expect me to sleep with you," she quipped.

He laughed. "Fair enough."

CREED
by *Phoenix Daniels*

CHAPTER 15
TAYLOR

After fighting through a crowd of reporters to get inside of her own home, all Taylor wanted was a drink, a hot bath, and believe it or not, Victor. When she saw her face on the front page of that paper, she should have run screaming from him. It wasn't that she thought it was his fault. After all, he didn't write the story or take the pictures. However, the expectation of privacy while dating the governor of Illinois was more than a little naive. If she didn't want to live under a microscope, she should have ended things with Victor. But somehow, she knew that she couldn't. That man did something to her. He put it on her good; in fact, better than any other man before him. Victor made her feel beautiful and sexy. He was all man, tall, thick, and dangerously handsome.

Taylor poured herself a glass of Pinot Noir and walked over to the sofa. She plopped down and grabbed her phone. She called her dad to cancel their trip. To her surprise, he never mentioned the article. She was thankful because she knew that he read the newspaper religiously every morning. He had to have seen the article, along with the derogatory headline. He was surely trying to save Taylor the embarrassment of explaining it. She studied

CREED
by *Phoenix Daniels*

her phone and debated whether or not she should return some of the many calls that she'd ignored. Deciding against it, she called Victor instead. When he didn't answer, she tossed her cellular on the sofa, went into her bedroom and plopped face down on her bed.

After ten minutes of inhaling his scent from her comforter, Taylor decided to get up, take a shower and shampoo her hair. Washing her hair would be the perfect distraction since it was long thick and completely natural. Combing it out and twisting it was bound to take at least an hour. After that, she'd find something else to occupy her time and keep her from obsessing about the lie that had been printed for all of Chicagoland to see.

****

Taylor stood in front of her bathroom mirror and twisted a section of her hair into a Bantu knot. She was wearing her old SIU t-shirt and a pair of shorts, thinking of how simple life was when she was in college. At that time, her entire life consisted of school and parties. It was college where she'd met Darin, her ex-husband. He was the dark chocolate, fine as hell, campus playboy that she thought that she had tamed. He was an affectionate, attentive boyfriend that wasn't ashamed to profess his undying

CREED
by *Phoenix Daniels*

love for her. So when he proposed at their graduation, Taylor felt as if she had won a prize. She jumped at the chance to marry him. However, shortly after the I do's were said, the affection stopped.

With her parent's marriage as an example, divorce was never an option for her. But, apparently, the union between Taylor's parents didn't mean two shits to Darin when he came home from work one day and told her that his mistress was pregnant and that he was leaving her. It was a part of Taylor's life that she wished that she could erase. But since she couldn't, and since she heard the sound of her front door opening and closing, she shoved all thoughts of her disastrous marriage and Darin back in the past where they belonged.

Taylor left the bathroom and walked down the hall. She entered the living room to find it empty.

"Hello," she called out.

"I'm in the kitchen!"

Taylor relaxed at the sound of Maria's voice. She walked into the kitchen and leaned over the breakfast bar, watching Maria help herself to her wine.

"They still out there?" Taylor asked.

"Yep. Oh, and, if I were you, I wouldn't turn on the TV."

"The TV?"

CREED
by *Phoenix Daniels*

Taylor was mortified. She hadn't even thought about the television media.

"Girl, yeah. They damn near on the verge of a prayer vigil for your poor innocent husband."

"Ughhhh... Fuck me," Taylor groaned, covering her face.

"There's a bright side," Maria offered.

"Yeah? What's that?"

"You look amazing in those pictures. Your ass is making a statement all by itself," Maria chuckled.

"Oh my God! I can't believe this bull-"

Taylor's rant was cut short when she heard the click of the lock on her front door. Taylor hurried into the living room in a panic. She wasn't afraid for her safety. She was seconds away from her weapon, and Maria was definitely packing. Her panic was sparked by the fact that the only other people that had a key to her house were her parents, and she wasn't ready to face them. To her relief, it was Kenyatta that entered.

"Hey," she said as she turned to lock the door.

"Kena, how did you get a key to my house?"

"You haven't figured out just how resourceful I am yet?" she responded with a smile.

Taylor didn't respond. She was not amused.

"How did you get a key to my house?" Taylor repeated.

CREED
by *Phoenix Daniels*

"Oh, calm down," she said, looking between Taylor and Maria. "Collier still had your keys. He said that he forgot to give them back. I took the liberty of using them because I was getting swarmed by reporters."

Taylor hadn't given her keys a second thought. "Oh."

"Kena, this is my friend and partner, Maria Mendez. Maria, Kenyatta is Victor's personal assistant."

"Please call me Kena. Everyone outside of work calls me Kena," Kenyatta insisted.

"Kena, would you like a glass of wine?" Maria offered.

"Maria, I would kill for a glass of wine."

"Come on. We're in the kitchen," Taylor gestured with a wave of her hand.

As Maria poured, Taylor asked, "So, what's up? What brings you by?"

"Well," Kenyatta hesitated a second before blurting, "I'm here to get you and take you back to the penthouse."

Taylor frowned. "What? Why would I go back to the penthouse? The media would have a field day with that."

"Taylor, just in case you haven't noticed, you could be staying on the moon, and they'll still have their field day."

"Victor said that he was coming over here. Have you talked to him?"

CREED
by *Phoenix Daniels*

Kenyatta knitted her brows and looked at Taylor as if she had just asked to most ridiculous question ever.

"Of course, I've talked to him."

"Can't you tell him that I'll stay inside until I have no choice but to leave the house and that I'll see him when he gets here?"

"Mm mmph," Kenyatta said, shaking her head. "I can't tell him that. Coming to get you was my idea. Taylor, he's the governor. I'm sure you understand that now that your address is public knowledge, there are some security issues. Besides, the governor had to go to Springfield to put out a few fires."

Taylor walked out of the kitchen without responding. She went and got the glass of wine that she'd left in her room and finished it in one gulp. She headed back into the kitchen with every intention on refilling the glass, at least, four more times.

"Taylor, I need you to pack a bag."

"Kena, I don't want to go out there," Taylor said, waving at the window. "I don't wanna go back to Victor's apartment so that those bastards can be all in my personal business."

Kenyatta's expression became sympathetic. "Taylor, sweetheart, that ship has sailed. Those bastards out there and those bastards at the penthouse are already in your personal business. And, I'm sorry to say... as soon as you fucked the governor of Illinois, not once, twice, or even three times, you became news."

Taylor could tell that Kenyatta was attempting to deliver her harsh words with as much patience as possible.

"The only thing that you can do now," she offered. "...is handle the situation with the dignity of the strong, classy sister that you are."

"She's right," Maria added with a shrug, before taking a sip from her glass.

"Fine," Taylor relented. "I'll pack a bag."

"Thank God," Kenyatta said with a chuckle. "If you had said no, Governor Creed swore that he'd come over, throw you over his shoulder, and carry you out of the house, media be damned."

"Damn, I love that man," Maria mumbled under her breath.

CHAPTER 16

CREED

After several face-to-face meetings and fielding call after call from campaign contributors, Victor realized that he hadn't heard from his biggest, most important benefactor. He pushed the intercom button.

"Yes, Governor Creed?"

"Lisa, can you get Jack Storm on the line, please?"

"Yes, sir."

A few minutes later, the phone rang in his office.

"Creed," he announced as he answered.

"Please hold for Mr. Storm," a female voice instructed.

Victor was placed on hold for at least three minutes. He drummed his fingers on his desk and waited, not so patiently, for Jack to come to the phone.

"Governor, how are you?" Jack's voice boomed through the line.

"Things could be better, but I'm getting it together."

"Yeah, I get that."

"You know only Jack Storm would have the balls to leave the governor of Illinois on hold," Victor chuckled.

CREED
by *Phoenix Daniels*

"Sorry, I was in the middle of making that million dollars that you're gonna need for your re-election campaign."

"Speaking of that... I just wanted to make sure that the recent media coverage hasn't cost me your support."

"She married, Victor?" he asked without mincing words.

"No, divorced. She's been divorced for years. The story is pure bullshit."

"Then you can count on my support."

Losing Jack's financial support would be detrimental to Victor's re-election campaign. Attempting to hide the relief in his voice, Victor replied, "Thanks, Jack."

"Now, Governor Creed, can I count on your support?"

"And what does that entail?" Victor asked cautiously.

"Well, as you know, my wife hosts an annual benefit to raise money for Sickle Cell Anemia. If the governor could attend and say a few words, it would do wonders for spreading awareness and raising funds for the charity."

"I'd be happy to make an appearance and say a few words."

"That would be most appreciated, Governor. Victoria will be ecstatic. And you know what they say...'happy wife, happy life.'"

"Yeah, that's what they say," Victor chuckled. "I gotta take this call. Send me the info."

"It's on the way."

CREED
by *Phoenix Daniels*

"Very good. We'll talk later."

"Later," Jack said before ending the call.

Victor stared at the phone, fully aware that he was just blackmailed by the billionaire. But Victor didn't care because all he could think of was Taylor. She couldn't have been happy with being attacked by the media solely based off her association with him. It was Tuesday, and he hadn't seen her since Saturday morning. He was still in Springfield, and although he was missing her, he found a strange comfort in knowing that she was sleeping in his bed every night. And even though they talked on the phone and through FaceTime throughout the entire weekend, it wasn't the same as having her in his arms or spooning her at night.

Admittedly, Victor was more than a little concerned about her returning to work. She'd told him that she'd spent the entire shift at police headquarters being questioned by Internal Affairs about the shooting. She assured him that she was represented by counsel, and all had gone well. But tonight, she was to return to the street, so Victor made arrangements to be back in Chicago in case she needed him. Though Taylor kept up a brave front, he knew that she was nervous about returning to the district.

A knock and the opening of the door shifted his focus from Taylor to Lisa, who was hurrying to his desk.

CREED
by *Phoenix Daniels*

"What is it?"

"The paper, sir," Lisa responded, smiling.

She sat the paper on his desk and left. Victor looked at the headline. It read: **GOVERNOR'S GIRLFRIEND NOT MARRIED.**

Victor read the article. It described Taylor as a smart, beautiful, tough, decorated female cop. It went on to say that, according to sources close to the governor, he was totally smitten, and he hadn't been as happy since before he lost his wife. The article had definitely painted a different picture of Taylor, and instead of a paparazzi photo like the last article, the paper used her official police photo. She was smiling beautifully and wearing her dress uniform. Her thick curly hair was in a tight bun in the back of her head.

She's so gorgeous, he thought as he reached for his phone.

"Yes, Governor?" Lisa answered.

"Send Renee Griffin a bottle of Veuve Clicquot. I heard somewhere that that was her favorite."

"Yes, sir," she responded. Victor could hear the smile in her voice.

CREED
by *Phoenix Daniels*

Renee had fixed Kara's mess, and he was grateful. But in the back of his mind, he knew that it wasn't going to be the last time that Taylor's name would be in the newspaper.

CREED
by *Phoenix Daniels*

TAYLOR

Taylor managed to get through roll call without any of the typical snide comments about her being a rat. She and Maria had gotten a few strange looks when they entered the station, but no one confronted them. Taylor leaned against the wall and waited as Maria signed out their radios and car keys.

"Hey, Taylor," a voice called from behind.

Taylor, recognizing the voice, turned around to see Candace Wallace walking out of the locker room.

"Hey, Candace. Wassup?"

Candace was a pretty, blonde, and well liked officer that Taylor had met in the police academy. She worked the day shift, and she was getting off. She was still wearing her uniform, but she'd thrown a White Sox jersey over her uniform shirt.

"Not too much. Same 'ol shit. It's hot, it's Chicago, so it's busy. We had three shootings in Roseland and one in Morgan Park. And, hell, that's only the South Side. I don't even wanna know what went down out west."

"Lord," Taylor said, shaking her head.

Candace moved closer to Taylor. Lowering her voice, she asked, "Did you know that Gore was stripped of his police powers yesterday?"

CREED
by *Phoenix Daniels*

"Naw. I hadn't heard."

"Girl, he went kicking and screaming."

"I bet."

"Yeah, but his partner's been talking big shit about you and Maria to anybody that'll listen; making all kinds of threats," she said with a frown.

"That asshole is barely off of probation. He don't wanna mess with me. Girl, he saw his partner gun that boy down for no reason and outright lied about it. It's only a matter of time before they strip his ass too."

"Just watch your back and be careful out there," Candace warned.

Taylor smiled at her concern. "Yes, ma'am," she responded.

"All right," Candace said with a nod. "I'll see you later."

Taylor watched Candace until she disappeared around the corner.

"Wassup there?" Maria asked, handing her a radio.

"Jim got stripped, and his partner is talking shit."

"Girl, ain't nobody thinking about his little punk ass. Come on; let's hit the street before they call our asses."

Taylor stuffed the radio in the holder and snapped the microphone to her shoulder. She followed Maria out of the back door. They walked through a sea of squad cars until they found

CREED
by *Phoenix Daniels*

the one that was assigned to them. Maria tossed Taylor the keys and walked around to the passenger side.

"What are we having for lunch today?" Taylor asked as she unlocked the door.

"Mexican," Maria responded. "We're going to my house for lunch."

"Yay!" Taylor squealed, hopping into the driver's seat.

But the tiny bit of excitement that she was experiencing disappeared at the site of a large dead rat hanging from the rear-view mirror. Maria screamed in horror and jumped from the vehicle, but Taylor remained calm. She wasn't horrified; she was furious. She pulled a pair of latex gloves out of her pocket, put them on, and detached the rat from the rear-view mirror.

"What the hell are you doing?" Maria asked when Taylor walked around the car carrying the large rat.

Taylor ignored her and marched back to the station. She walked in the back door and hurled the rodent into the station. The flying rat bounced when it hit the floor, and then slid across the linoleum. Female, as well as male police officers, leaped, screaming hysterically, trying to avoid the rat.

"IF ANYBODY GOT SOMETHING TO SAY TO ME, SAY IT TO MY FUCKING FACE!" Taylor shouted before storming out of the station.

CREED

by *Phoenix Daniels*

CHAPTER 17

TAYLOR

Taylor relaxed against the pillow and moaned at the exquisite pleasure she was getting from Victor's expert fingers. After the day she had, he was trying to alleviate her tension with a foot massage.

"It drives me crazy when you make those noises," he said in a seductive tone.

"Go crazy, baby," she teased.

Victor stood from his seated position at the foot of Taylor's bed and climbed over her. "You talked me into it," he said with a sexy smirk.

Taylor's giggle was cut short when his full lips connected to hers. She loved his lips. With them, he had loved every inch of her body. The way he kissed her was mind blowing. Taylor melted against the pillow, putting all of her concerns about work on the back burner and allowed him to take her to a better place.

Victor severed their connection, just long enough to shed them both of their clothing and grab a golden packet. But within a matter of seconds, their lips were fused together once again. He nudged her legs apart with his feet and massaged her engorged clit. Taylor's breath hitched as he ignited a bundle of nerves. He began to place light kisses down her neck, then her chest, until he latched onto her nipple. The synchronous stimulation of her clit and nipple was driving Taylor to the brink of madness.

"Umm-hmm... Yes," she groaned.

Taylor drove herself against his talented fingers until she completely shattered. She took a few seconds to recover before pushing Victor to his back. She mounted him and stared down at his beautiful green eyes, his perfectly sculpted torso, and then his big back-breaking dick and whispered, "Damn," mainly to herself.

He smiled, exposing a beautiful set of dimples. Wanting to consume every bit of him, she lowered herself and licked his hard dick before inserting it into her mouth. She gently massaged his balls, sealed her lips around his shaft, and sucked his dick rhythmically slow.

"Damn, sweetness," he moaned. "So good, baby."

His moans became louder and the muscles in his thighs tensed. Victor's demeanor changed. He grabbed two fistfuls of Taylor's hair and aggressively guided her up and down on his dick.

"Yeah, baby!" he growled loudly, pushing harder and deeper.

CREED

by *Phoenix Daniels*

To Taylor, Victor's aggression was a major turn-on. She found herself moaning and groaning along with him. She mimicked the movement of her lips and roughly stroked his dick with her hand, earning a fierce growl.

Victor released her hair and grabbed her head, stilling her movement.

"Babe, you're gonna make me cum," he warned.

"I want you to."

"Not this time, baby," he said, pulling her to straddle him.

"No, baby, I'm fucking you tonight. I wanna be inside of you, wanna feel your heat wrapped around my cock, wanna hear and feel the wetness of your tight pussy."

He raised her enough to slide inside. Taylor held her breath as she stretched to accommodate his size. Once completely impaled, she was able to exhale. Victor's hands moved to her hips, and Taylor began to ride. She rose and fell on his dick, savoring every inch of him. They fell into a synchronized push and pull that had Taylor panting uncontrollably. Victor tightened his grip on her hips and drove deeper and deeper, causing Taylor to cry out in ecstasy.

"Ohhhh! Ohhhh... Gotdamn... Yesss! I'm cumming, Victor!" she screamed as she erupted.

CREED
by *Phoenix Daniels*

On the verge of collapsing, her hands fell to the pillow. He grabbed the sides of her face and pulled her mouth to his. Taylor caressed his tongue with her own, moaning into his mouth as he fucked her from below. She was already climbing toward another orgasm. Victor palmed both of her breasts and toyed with her nipples, prompting Taylor to ride harder. She slammed herself down on his dick, over and over, until her own sweat was running down her back.

Tearing his mouth away from hers, Victor began sucking and licking her tits, alternating between both.

"Victor, baby, your dick is so fucking good to me," Taylor purred. "So fucking good."

"That's because this is my pussy, sweetness," he growled, before flipping her over on her back.

"This pussy belongs to me. Doesn't it, Taylor?" he grunted.

"Yes, baby," Taylor admitted.

He climbed on top and entered her quickly, positioning both of her legs over his shoulders, and the pounding commenced. Victor knew exactly how to do her; when to make love to her, and when to fuck the stress out of her. He always seemed to know what she needed, and he always gave it to her.

His thrusts frenzied.

"Dammit, baby! I'm... cu-cumming," he choked.

CREED
by *Phoenix Daniels*

He slammed into her one last time and stilled. Taylor could actually feel his dick pulsing hot cum into her.

****

Taylor was relaxing against Victor's chest, realizing that there was no place else that she'd rather be; not just at his penthouse, but in his arms. She rubbed the soft hairs on his chest as his fingers roamed through her hair.

"What is it with you and my hair?" she asked, breaking the silence in the room.

"What do you mean?"

"You know what I mean. You're always asking me to take it out of the ponytail, and you're always playing in it."

"I just really like it. It's different," he admitted.

Taylor was puzzled. "Different? Victor, you've been with Black women before."

"Yes, and, like I said, your hair is different."

"How?"

"Well, it's big, and well... um... feral. Sometimes, when your hair is free, you remind me of a sexier version of Pam Grier."

Taylor broke out laughing. "Victor, you got a thing for Pam Grier?"

CREED
by *Phoenix Daniels*

"Shit, didn't everyone?" he chuckled.

"Yeah, Black men."

"Taylor, baby, if you think that, you're bat shit crazy," he quipped.

Of course, Taylor was only teasing. She was well aware that a photo of Pam Grier was damn near every man's masturbation material, Black or White.

"So, baby, what you do think about going on our first public outing?" he asked, changing the subject.

"Huh?"

"I have to attend a charity event next week, and I'd like you to accompany me."

"What kind of charity even?"

"It's a black-tie ball for Sickle Cell."

"Victoria's thing?" Taylor asked.

"That's right; you do know Victoria Storm. I almost forgot. Yes, it's her event. Her husband blackmailed me into speaking."

"Sounds like the perfect man for Victoria. She hounded me for weeks to stand in one of her bachelorette auctions one year."

"And you did it?"

"Hell yeah," she chuckled. "There ain't no telling Victoria Storm no."

CREED
by *Phoenix Daniels*

"Is that so?" he asked, amused that *anyone* can force Taylor into doing something she didn't want to do.

"Yep. That was when she met her husband. He bid a million dollars for one date with her. At least, I think that's how they met. Can you believe that?"

"I can," he responded, kissing the top of her head. "There's no way that I'd let someone outbid me for you."

"Ha," she joked. "What if it was Jack? He's a damn billionaire."

"Taylor, I'm not exactly poor. I would probably be a formidable opponent against Jack Storm in a bidding war. And if his bid was too high for me to beat, I'd hit my brothers up for loot. And if that didn't work, I'd just shoot him."

Taylor giggled and playfully slapped his chest.

"Babe?"

"Hmm?"

"Why don't you ever talk about your wife?" she asked, totally changing the subject.

"Why don't you ever talk about your husband?" he asked, redirecting the question.

"I got married. I got divorced. End of story."

"I got married. She died. End of story."

CREED
by *Phoenix Daniels*

She huffed, as if his reply wasn't as evasive as her own. "Victor, do you want us to know each other for real?"

"I do, Sweetness."

Taylor's eyes narrowed as she studied him. His answer was short, but he seemed sincere.

"I have an idea," he added.

"Why don't we take a road trip? My brothers are flying in, in a few weeks. My family has a lake house in Benton Harbor, Michigan. They've planned a family getaway. It's a couple hour's drive, so we can talk about all the stuff that we've never talked about."

Taylor couldn't hide her surprise. "You want me to meet your family?"

"Yes, of course. Taylor, you're the woman in my life. I never thought I'd feel like this, but, I want my brothers to get on your nerves, just like they get on mine, and I want my mother to gossip and share old recipes with you."

Taylor climbed on top of his big body. "Damn, I'm really in a relationship with the governor, huh?"

"Yeah, sweetness. You're the governor's lady," he confirmed with a kiss to her lips. "The time for hiding is over. You're mine, and I want the world to know."

"Why?" she asked.

CREED
by *Phoenix Daniels*

"It's simple, really. I don't want any other asshole thinking for one minute that he can have you. That ass is mine," he responded with a sexy smirk.

"Well, you are now in possession of a whole lot of ass," she joked, cuffing her own behind.

Covering her hands with his, he confirmed, "That I am."

CREED
by *Phoenix Daniels*

CHAPTER 18
TAYLOR

Taylor stood in front of the garage as the door raised and waited for her baby to come into view; her black and yellow Ducati Monster. It was warm out, but not too hot, a perfect day for riding.

She walked her bike out of the garage and closed the garage door. Taylor adjusted her leather shin guard and threw her leg over the bike. When she kicked the motor, she could instantly feel the powerful hum between her thighs. The vibrations were exhilarating. She slid her helmet over her head and eased out of her driveway.

Once on the street, she kicked it up a couple of gears and picked up speed. While riding through street traffic, Taylor kept a moderate speed. But when she hit the expressway, she was able to open it up and truly ride the Monster. She weaved between the cars until she made it downtown.

It was lunchtime, and there was a lot of traffic downtown. She was meeting Victor at his apartment for lunch, and she arrived just as he was. He exited the back seat of a dark SUV in a crisp black suit. His thick dark hair was blowing in the wind, and his beautiful green eyes were covered by dark shades. Victor

CREED
by *Phoenix Daniels*

exuded nothing but power and masculinity. Everything about him screamed "MAN." He was a sight to see.

Taylor pulled behind the SUV and killed the engine. She kicked out the stand and pulled off her helmet. Victor narrowed his eyes and studied Taylor, making sure that it was really her.

After climbing off the bike, she dropped her helmet on the seat and walked over to him. He leaned down and gave her a soft peck.

"You never cease to amaze me, young lady," he told her, patting her leather clad ass.

"All right now, you better cut that out before it winds up on the front page of the paper," Taylor warned with a giggle.

"Fuck the paper," he said, giving her another swat. "How much time we got?"

"I gotta be at work at four."

"That gives us a couple of hours. Let's go," he ordered, pulling her toward Storm Tower.

****

Taylor rode in silence, thinking about the way that Victor had put it on her earlier that day. She and Maria were patrolling their beat. There was still tension at work, but Taylor and Maria

CREED
by *Phoenix Daniels*

thankfully hadn't had any more dead rodents planted in their squad car. They were actually having a peaceful and uneventful night, no strange calls all night. But that didn't mean that Taylor didn't have concerns. Maria seemed to be down all week. She just wasn't her fiery, vibrant self. She hadn't gushed over her family, and whenever Taylor brought them up, Maria would grunt and become obviously dismissive.

"What's the deal, Maria?" Taylor asked, breaking the silence. "What's up with you?"

"Huh? I'm good."

"Naw, uh uh, don't do that. I know you, and you haven't been yourself. What's going on?"

Tears began to fall as Maria pulled to the curb. Taylor grasped her shoulder gently, wanting to bring comfort to her friend.

"What's wrong, sweetie?"

"Michael wants a divorce," she blurted.

Taylor gasped. "What? No!... But y'all seemed so happy."

"I thought we were happy. That is until he came home from work and asked me for a divorce."

Taylor clasped Maria's hand. She couldn't believe what she was hearing.

"So, you didn't see this coming at all?" Taylor asked.

CREED
by *Phoenix Daniels*

"No," she sobbed. "I thought we had a great marriage; thought we were in love, Taylor.

"Did he say why?"

Maria dropped her head in shame as her tears flowed freely. Taylor had never once seen her friend cry. Seeing her in that state was causing tears to well in her own eyes.

"He said that he was in love with another woman."

"No, Maria. Are you serious?"

Maria nodded.

"That bastard!" Taylor hissed.

"Said the hours I work left him lonely. Said he has needs. Taylor, I swear to God that I fucked that man every time he wanted it. It didn't matter how tired I was; I made sure that he was taken care of. I made sure that he and the girls always had a home cooked meal, clean clothes, and a lot of love."

"I know you did, Maria."

"How could he do this to me?!" Maria cried.

Confined in the car, Taylor managed to wrap an arm around Maria's shoulder and pulled her as close as she could.

"I tried to be a good wife; tried to make him happy," Maria whimpered.

"Maria, you are a good wife. He's an asshole to leave you and the girls. He's using your job as an excuse to justify himself

CREED
by *Phoenix Daniels*

for fucking some other chick. Don't you dare blame yourself for his bullshit."

Maria nodded and wiped the tears from her face.

"Head back to the station. We're leaving early today," Taylor told her.

"Why?"

"Because we're gonna get drunk. No, not drunk, but slapped, twisted, shit-faced, fucked up. I mean straight up white girl wasted. You down for that?"

"Hell yeah," Maria murmured, forcing a smile.

CREED

by *Phoenix Daniels*

CREED

Victor massaged his temple, thinking of how stubborn his Taylor was. She had called to tell him that she was leaving work early and that she and Maria were going out drinking. Apparently, Maria was having some issues at home; issues that must have been an issue for Taylor as well, because when she called, Victor could hear the anguish in her voice. He'd suggested that they leave their cars at work and allow Collier to take them where they wanted to go, but of course, Taylor said no. So his suggestion ended up becoming a request, then an insistence, then ultimately, an order. Taylor obviously didn't like being told what to do, but Victor couldn't have given less than a damn as long as she was safe.

She eventually gave in.

As if he was giving her a choice.

It was Friday, not that it mattered to Victor. The job as governor kept him busy seven days a week, but the Sickle Cell Ball was the next day, and he was actually looking forward to it. It was going to be his first public outing with Taylor. He wanted to rip off the bandage, so to speak; making their relationship public. He wanted to get the news out his way so that it could no longer be newsworthy. He couldn't believe that he was so eager

CREED
by *Phoenix Daniels*

for the world to know about a woman... after Rosemary. But of course, their relationship was only formed for promotional purposes. And ever since her death, his privacy was extremely important to him. Now, because of Taylor, he needed the news of their relationship to become old news so that things could get back to normal for her. He was thankful that the media hadn't already driven her away.

Victor put in a quick call to Collier, telling him that he was on Taylor duty. Then he called Gregor and arranged his own transportation. It had been a long day of meetings filled with the mayor of Chicago and smaller Illinois cities, explaining why their failure to manage their city's budgets wasn't their fault. They, apparently, thought that city funding miraculously fell from a money producing tree. The explanations/excuses were exhausting.

He grabbed his jacket from the back of his chair and prepared to leave. Relaxing at his apartment while waiting for Taylor to come in and give him some drunk pussy was Victor's idea of heaven.

"Governor Creed, your dad is here," Kena announced through the intercom.

Well, drunk pussy would have been heaven.

"Send him in."

CREED
by *Phoenix Daniels*

Victor Creed Sr. stepped into Victor's office. He was wearing a crisp gray suit that flattered his tall, solid frame. For a man his age, Victor's dad was still turning heads. The man didn't have so much as one grey strand in his hair. And when he smiled, which was rare, his green eyes sparkled like a man half his age.

Good genes, Victor thought. And he prayed that he'd inherited them.

"Hello, Son," he said as he sat without an invitation.

"Dad, how are you?"

"Good, Son; good. Just coming by to see how you're doing," Victor Sr. responded with a smile.

Victor narrowed his eyes at his dad. He wasn't buying it. "No, really, what's the real reason for this unexpected visit?"

"Can't a dad come by and check on his eldest son?"

"Yes, Father, but I suspect that's not why you're here."

With no further hesitation, he asked. "What's with you and this Black girl?"

Victor didn't like the way his dad phrased his question. "What's with me and this *Black* girl?" he repeated.

"Yes, what's this all about, Son?

"We're dating, Dad. We're together, and her name is Taylor…Taylor Montgomery, not Black girl."

"Is it serious?" he asked, disregarding Victor's tone.

CREED
by *Phoenix Daniels*

"She's important to me."

"Okay. I can't wait to meet this important woman of yours."

Victor rubbed his temple. Surely, that wasn't all his father had to say; not the man that had had his life and wife mapped out since he was a child.

"Really?" Victor asked.

"Really," Victor senior assured.

"Anyway, she'll ensure more Black votes come election time."

The statement, to Victor, was offensive. "Dad, I'm not with Taylor for votes."

"Yes, Son, I know. I was just pointing it out. I'm sure she's a lovely young lady."

"That she is, Dad," Victor confirmed. "You got dinner plans?"

"Nope."

"Perfect. Let's head to my apartment. I'll make us a couple of steaks."

"Well, I'm not one to turn down a steak. Let's go."

CREED
by *Phoenix Daniels*

CHAPTER 19
TAYLOR

"Hey, Gregor," Taylor squealed as she stumbled out of the elevator.

After studying her a few seconds, he smiled. "Hello, Taylor. I see you ain't feelin' no pain," he chuckled.

"I'm goooood," she sang.

When Taylor walked into the penthouse, she could hear Nickelback's S.E.X. blaring from the rec room. Sex was exactly what she had in mind, so she took it as a subliminal message to shed her clothing. She danced her way into the rec room, leaving a trail of clothes behind. She entered, fully prepared to put it on her sexy man.

"Hi, honey. I'm hoooome," she sang in her best seductive voice.

But, unfortunately, she found herself standing butt ass naked in front of an older Victor lookalike. Drunk and stunned, Taylor stood frozen, staring at the man that was staring at her.

"Taylor!" Victor shouted, snapping her from her daze.

She attempted to cover as much as she could as she backed out of the room. She ran to the bedroom and searched for the t-shirt and sweats that Victor had given.

CREED
by *Phoenix Daniels*

After dressing quickly, she began to pace the floor. Instantly and completely sober, whatever buzz that she may have had was gone.

"Oh my God. Oh my God. Oh my God," she was chanting to herself until Victor entered the room. "Oh God, babe, I am soooo sorry. I didn't know you had company. Is that your dad? Fuck! Of course, that's your dad. Oh God, I just stood there. Victor, your father saw me naked! I'm so sorry."

Victor grabbed Taylor's shoulders and looked deep into her eyes. "Baby, calm down. It's okay. It's fine."

"Victor, I am so embarrassed. I could just die."

"Sweetness, it's fine," he assured.

"How am I supposed to face him?"

Taylor didn't think she could be more horrified.

"Well, you're going to have to figure it out, because he's waiting to meet you."

"I can't, Victor," Taylor insisted while shaking her head.

"You can and you will. Besides, I suspect that my dad has seen a naked woman once or twice," he chuckled, attempting to put her at ease.

Victor gently kissed her forehead and walked over to the drawer that he had assigned her. He fished out a bra. His eyes grazed over her breast, causing Taylor to look down at herself.

CREED
by *Phoenix Daniels*

Her hardened nipples were poking through the thin material of the t-shirt. She looked up into Victor's smoldering gaze.

"Sweetness, tonight I'm gonna have a go at those. But for now, I need you to put this on," he said with a sexy smirk, handing her the bra.

Taylor pulled the shirt over her head and took the bra. Victor's moss colored irises seemed to darken. He caressed her bare breast and let out a feral groan before stepping back.

"Woman, in a minute you're gonna make me say to hell with the old man. Put your clothes on and meet us in the recreation room," he told her as he backed out of the bedroom.

He was smiling that double dimpled smile that made him look young and mischievous. In such a short time, Victor had become very important to Taylor. Her insides fluttered whenever he was close. She had often found herself counting down the hours and minutes of the day until it was time to see him. Taylor went to bed thinking of him, and he was her first thought when she awakened every morning. She slipped on the bra and threw the t-shirt over her head. She walked over to the mirror and checked her hair before reluctantly exiting the bedroom.

When she entered the rec room, Victor Sr. and Jr. were laughing loudly, each nursing a drink. Victor Sr. looked up at her and smiled. Taylor's face was burning with shame, but she returned his smile with her own shy grin. He placed his drink on the table and stood.

"Hello, Miss Montgomery. It's nice to meet you," he said, walking toward her with his hand out.

Taylor met him halfway and extended her hand. "It's nice to meet you, Senator Creed. I…Um…I apologize for...” Taylor stuttered.

Creed Sr. gently squeezed her hand. "Nonsense, it's forgotten. Well, not completely forgotten," he said with a wink that somehow made Taylor feel a tiny bit less embarrassed. "Come, young lady, let's sit down and get to know each other," he said, leading her to the sofa.

CREED

Victor was relaxing in the tub, holding Taylor close, and thinking of his father's visit. Watching Taylor charm his dad gave Victor one more reason to be impressed with her. Victor Sr. usually wore a suit of armor that wasn't easily penetrated. He'd settled into a comfortable conversation with Taylor about everything from her job to fishing with her dad. He'd even teased her about her naked entrance. Victor Sr. never teased. Victor tried to remember a time when his father had actually had a personal conversation with Rosemary. He couldn't remember one single incident.

Other than another man's eyes on Taylor's beautiful body, the introduction had gone well. Before leaving, he'd even told Taylor that he was looking forward to seeing her at the family outing the next week. Victor was pleasantly surprised that they'd hit it off so well.

"You're too quiet. What are you thinking about?" Taylor asked, interrupting his thoughts.

"You. I'm always thinking about you," he admitted.

"Yeah, I know what you mean. I think about you all day every day."

"Oh yeah?" Victor said, lifting her by the waist.

CREED
by *Phoenix Daniels*

"Let's get out of here and go to bed so I can give you some more to think about."

"Shi-id, let's go."

CREED
by *Phoenix Daniels*

CHAPTER 20
TAYLOR

At the sound of the ringing doorbell, Taylor crossed the living room and inhaled a deep breath before opening the door. She was preparing herself for the earful that she was sure to get.

She exhaled and opened the door.

"Oh, so you now need me, huh? You've been avoiding me for months. Hell, the only time I get to see you is when your ass is in the paper," her sister ranted as she entered the house, pulling a rack of dresses behind her. "But now that you need something from me, I'm suddenly graced with your presence. But it's cool. I'm not important. Obviously not since I had to find out that you were fucking the governor from the Sun-Times."

Taylor had no rebuttal. After all, Nicole was right. She had shut her family out, not knowing how they would react to her seeing Victor. She remained silent as she went to close the door.

"Don't close it. Momma's right behind me," Nicole said with a devious smirk.

"Oh, you bitch," Taylor mumbled under her breath.

"What? She wanted to come. I'm supposed to say no? You're gonna have to face her someday. Why not today?"

CREED
by *Phoenix Daniels*

Before Taylor could respond, Martha Montgomery walked in, juggling several shoe boxes. Taylor grabbed the boxes from her mother's arms and sat them on the floor.

Taylor then gave her mother a hug.

"Hey, Ma. You look so pretty."

And she did. She was wearing a smart, grey, figure flattering pantsuit and black pumps. Her mom had beautiful dark skin, hazel eyes, and bouncy shoulder-length hair.

"Thank you," she replied curtly.

Taylor, not wasting any time, started groveling right away. "Ma, I'm sorry I've been avoiding you. I was just really embarrassed when that article came out. I was too scared to tell you that I was dating Victor. I didn't know how you'd respond. And I didn't know what it was that we were doing exactly. I'm real sorry, Mommy."

Martha grabbed both sides of Taylor's face and stared deep into her eyes. "Don't you ever be afraid to talk to me. You know damn well that you can talk to me about *anything*. Do you hear me?"

"Yes, Ma. I apologize."

Martha kissed Taylor's cheek and said, "You're forgiven."

"Thanks, Mommy."

CREED
by *Phoenix Daniels*

"That's it!" Nicole blurted. "She's forgiven just like that? If it were me, I'd a' been disowned."

"Child, hush and pull them damn dresses out."

Nicole pretended to pout as she flipped through the dress rack. Taylor laughed at her antics.

"Oh, and Taylor, if I were gonna be slutting it up with anybody, that fine ass man woulda been at the top of my list too," her mother smiled.

"Umm... Yuck," Nicole responded without looking up.

"How about you stick to 'slutting it up,' as you call it, with James Montgomery," Taylor remarked.

"Girl, I'm just saying," Martha chuckled. "The man is gorgeous."

"Kill me now," Taylor muttered, walking over to Nicole. "Can we just find me a dress for tonight?"

"Yep," Martha replied. "And while we do that, you're gonna tell us all about your new man."

✳✳✳✳

"Wow," Taylor gushed after opening the door for Kena. "You look amazing."

"Thanks," Kena responded after completing a twirl.

179

CREED
by *Phoenix Daniels*

She was wearing a strapless black ball gown that accentuated her every curve. Her long hair was pinned on one side by a beautiful red flower.

"I do believe, Miss Montgomery, that the governor is going to blow his top when he sees you tonight."

"You like?" Taylor asked while striking a pose.

"Girl, you look incredible."

"Well, thank you."

Miraculously, Taylor, her mom, and her sister had agreed on a gown. It was a form-fitting white gown made of satin with a square neckline and capped sleeves. Thank God for Nicole and her fancy job in fashion, because Taylor would never have been able to spend so much on a dress. She completed her ensemble with a pair of silver strappy stilettos and a silver clutch. Her mom and sister had loved the dress on her, but they were unified in their hatred of her hair. She wore it loose, letting her wild curls free. They did their very best to persuade her to pin it up. Their pleas fell on deaf ears because Victor loved her hair wild and free. And at some point, she intended on him digging his fingers in her scalp while riding her hard.

"You ready?" Kena asked. "I got champagne chilling in the limo."

"Yep, let's go."

CREED
by *Phoenix Daniels*

Taylor grabbed her keys from the table, and they were off.

It didn't take long for them to arrive at the Four Seasons on Michigan Avenue. This year, the Ball was to be held in their Grand Ballroom, instead of the Barrington Country Club. Maybe the country club was a bit gun-shy after a bomb went off at the last Sickle Cell Ball. It all worked out because the Four Seasons was absolutely breathtaking. When they pulled in front, Taylor noticed that there was actually a red carpet surrounded by reporters. She was immediately intimidated.

"Don't sweat it, lady. Hold your head up high. You're the governor's lady," Kenyatta encouraged, handing her another glass of champagne.

When Collier hopped out of the front seat, Taylor downed her champagne with one gulp and placed the glass in the holder.

Collier opened the door and helped Kena out of the limo.

"It's the governor's limo!" one reporter shouted when he saw Kena.

When Collier's hand entered the limo, Taylor took a deep cleansing breath and grabbed his hand. She stepped out, held her head high, and joined Kena on the red carpet. The flashing lights, from what seemed like a million cameras, were blinding. She smiled and followed Kena down the red carpet.

"Taylor, where's Governor Creed?" a reporter shouted.

CREED
by *Phoenix Daniels*

When others began to scream the same question, Kena leaned and whispered, "Smile and answer them."

"Really?" Taylor asked, praying that she was joking.

"Yes. Trust me."

Taylor turned to the reporters, brandishing her sweetest smile and said, "The governor had to finish up a little work. He's a very busy man, but he'll be here shortly."

She turned around and continued down the red carpet.

"You look beautiful, Taylor!" one shouted.

"Who are you wearing?!" shouted another.

Taylor and Kena entered the hotel and were immediately escorted to the ballroom. They were on time, and the place was already packed. She looked around at the elegant decor and beautifully designed tables. Each table had a centerpiece with floating white orchids. Taylor adored orchids. She had never been in a room so beautiful in all her life.

"This place is a palace," Taylor whispered to Kena.

"Oh my God, yes," Kena agreed.

"Well, gotdamn, Taylor. Girl, you look gooood."

Taylor turned, knowing that Victoria's flirting ass was behind her, but she didn't expect to see Natasha Walker, well Natasha *Storm* now, standing next to her.

"Tash!" Taylor shouted with excitement.

CREED
by *Phoenix Daniels*

"Wassup, Tay?" Natasha responded with excitement.

The ladies embraced, happy to see each other.

"Umm... Helloooo. I'm still here." Victoria grumbled.

"Girl, shut up," Taylor said. "I just saw yo' ass."

The ladies laughed. Well, all except for Victoria. She was now, focused on Kena. Taylor chuckled.

"Vic, Tasha, this is the governor's PA, Kenyatta," she announced.

"It's nice to meet you both," Kenyatta said, not taking her eyes off of Victoria, who in turn was still staring at her.

Oh shit. What's this?

"It's nice to meet you," Natasha intervened. "Please forgive my rude cousin," she added, staring at Victoria.

"She's forgiven," Kena responded quickly, still staring at Victoria.

"Jesus," Natasha grumbled.

"Where's your husband, Victoria?" Taylor asked, chastising.

"Trust me," Natasha assured. "If Jack comes over here, it's gonna get a lot worse."

Taylor couldn't suppress her laughter.

"So, Kenyatta, what do I have to do to convince you to participate in my bachelorette auction?" Victoria asked.

CREED
by *Phoenix Daniels*

Kenyatta smiled. "Victoria, I suspect that you could get me to do just about anything if you asked nicely."

"In that case, come with me. Let's get you a drink so that I can ask you nicely," Victoria said, rather seductively, Taylor noted.

Together, they walked away, leaving Taylor and Natasha staring at their backs.

"What the fuck just happened?" Taylor asked, with a chuckle.

"Storm Victoria."

"That girl hasn't changed a bit," Taylor said, shaking her head.

"I know. She's something else. Gotta love her, though. Come on. Let's go get a drink."

CREED

by *Phoenix Daniels*

CREED

Victor entered the ballroom and went on an immediate search for Taylor. The place was packed. It was funny how the Storm name and money attracted a multitude of wealthy social climbers. Finding her through the large crowd wasn't going to be easy, but Victor was determined.

As we weaved through the socialites, he continued to scan the room.

Then he found her.

The sight of her stopped him in his tracks. He wanted to make a smooth approach, but his feet were cemented to the floor. She had left him frozen. Taylor was a breathtaking vision in white. The dress she wore complimented everything that was beautiful about her body, and her hair was styled the way he loved it. Visions of her as a bride stunned Victor, and at that moment, he knew that he was done for.

"She got you stuck, huh?" Jack Storm mused.

"What?" he asked, still in somewhat of a daze.

"Here; drink this," Jack said, handing Victor a glass of champagne. "You look like you could use a drink. Seems like a piano just fell on you, but I don't blame you. She *is* a beauty."

CREED
by *Phoenix Daniels*

Victor knocked back the champagne and turned to Jack. "You just worry about *your* beauty. By the way, where is she, since you're over here gawking at what's mine?"

Victor pretended to scan the room for Victoria. "No doubt, she's probably somewhere with your hot assistant, convincing her to come home with us," Jack chuckled.

Victor stared at Jack, trying to gauge his seriousness, and he did not appear to be joking.

"No bullshit?"

"Nope," Jack responded, shaking his head.

"Damn, you lucky bastard."

"That I am," Jack replied, smiling.

"Yeah, so, you and your wife had better stay away from my woman."

Jack laughed and walked away.

Victor handed the empty glass to a passing waiter and made his way over to Taylor. When she spotted him, her face seemed to light up. Knowing that she was just as happy to see him as he was to see her, caused Victor's heart to swell. He pulled her in his arms and held her tight. Her soft body seemed to warm him on the inside. He kissed the top of her head and reluctantly released her.

"Taylor, your beauty leaves me speechless."

CREED
by *Phoenix Daniels*

"Thank you, baby. You're lookin' pretty damn fine yourself. I wanna take you home with me," she whispered.

"And you shall, Sweetness. But first, dance with me."

Victor led Taylor to the dance floor and pulled her close. She pressed her body against his and rested her head on chest. As they began to sway to the soft music, Victor inhaled the minty, spa-like scent of Taylor's hair. He held her tight, thinking that their bodies were like two pieces of a puzzle. Together, they fit perfectly. It was as if there was no one else in the room, and he enjoyed their "alone time" until the song ended. That was when the lights dimmed, and a spotlight hit Natasha on stage.

"Is she gonna sing?" Taylor asked.

Taylor seemed shocked. She thought that Natasha was always so quiet and shy. But there she stood, on stage, like a beautiful, confident siren. The Storms had picked well, but not one of them had a thing on Taylor.

Victor rubbed her back, realizing that he could have held her forever. And he would have if Victoria hadn't approached them. Her expression gave him pause. She was clearly disturbed as she placed her hand on Taylor's shoulder.

Taylor's voice was filled with concern. "What's wrong, Vic?"

CREED
by *Phoenix Daniels*

"I just heard about..." Victoria inhaled a deep breath as if she was struggling with her words.

"What, Vic? You heard about what?!"

Victor could hear the panic forming in Taylor's voice.

"It's Mendez," she said in a shaky voice. "She went on a burglary call. She... Taylor, she was shot."

CREED
by *Phoenix Daniels*

CHAPTER 21
TAYLOR

Taylor's suddenly found it difficult to breathe. Victor caught her when she momentarily lost her footing.

"Is she alive?" Taylor asked hopefully.

"I don't know, Taylor. One of the guys from my old team just told me that she was shot in the back while on a burglary call, and she's at Christ Hospital."

"I... I gotta go," Taylor said, standing upright.

She grabbed the bottom of her dress and bolted toward the exit. Although Victor had no problem keeping up with her, he tugged her arm and slowed her down for several reasons. One, she was wearing extremely tall heels. Two, if the press saw her running, they'd run right behind her, and the press was the last thing that Taylor needed to deal with. Thankfully, she slowed, allowing Victor to pull out his phone and call Collier. After instructing him to bring the car around to the rear of the hotel, he changed their course.

****

CREED
by *Phoenix Daniels*

Taylor's heels clicked loudly as she rushed through a crowd of nurses and cops to get to Maria.

"In there," one officer instructed.

Taylor walked over to Maria's room but stopped short at the door. She looked over at Victor, hoping to magically siphon some of his strength.

"It'll be okay, babe, I promise. I'll be right out here if you need me," he assured.

Taylor nodded, ignoring the fact that everyone was staring at the two of them and entered the room. Her heart stopped when she saw her friend lying in a hospital bed with her eyes taped shut and a machine breathing for her. She stood still and watched Maria's chest rise and fall every time the machine pushed air into her lungs. For some reason, she was afraid to approach the bed, but she knew that she had to. It was just too painful to see her partner that way. If only she'd taken off work and come to the ball like Taylor had asked. If only Taylor hadn't taken the day off, she would have had her partner's back.

If only...

Taylor walked over to Maria, swiped some of the tears from her own cheek, and took her hand. She prayed to God, pleading for a full recovery.

CREED

by *Phoenix Daniels*

"I'm not letting you go. You hear me, Maria?" Taylor whispered close to her ear. "You're gonna be okay."

"Taylor?" a voice called from behind, startling her.

She turned to find Michael, Maria's husband, standing in the doorway. His expression was grim, and he seemed truly distraught for a man that no longer loved his wife.

"She's gonna make it, right?" he asked, searching for reassurance.

"Of course, she is, but I didn't realize that you cared."

He narrowed his eyes and took a step toward Taylor. "Don't you ever fucking say that to me again!" he snapped. "I love my wife. Yeah, I fucked up, but I love my wife. So if you're gonna be here, keep your fucked up comments to yourself."

With that being said, he turned his back to Taylor and wiped tears from his face.

"Michael, she's gonna make it," Taylor said to his back.

Once fully composed, he crossed the room and sat in the chair next to Maria's bed.

Michael and Maria had been married for a long time, and Taylor knew nothing about the dynamics of their relationship; only what she'd heard from Maria. Before his indiscretion, they seemed very happy. Taylor decided that it would be best to mind her business and let them deal with their own marital issues.

CREED
by *Phoenix Daniels*

"Where are the kids?" she asked.

"They're at my sister's. Both of our parents are on their way."

"Do you need me to do anything?"

"Naw, I don't think so. I'm just waiting for them to take her into surgery."

She walked over to Michael and placed a reassuring hand on his shoulder. "Okay. I'm gonna go and grab some food for you guys, and I'll be back."

"Thanks, Taylor," he responded in sad tone.

After giving Maria a kiss to her forehead, Taylor left the room. Victor was across the hall in a huddle with Kena. Gregor and a small security detail were standing quietly in the background. The sound of the door closing prompted Victor and Kena to look up. Both of their faces were masked with concern. Victor opened his arms, and the simple gesture caused Taylor to break. She flew into his arms and began to ball hysterically. She just didn't have the amount of strength needed to bear the thought of losing Maria. She was so much more than a partner, so much more than a friend, she was like her other sister, the one that she saw more regularly and had more in common with.

"Shhh... She'll make it through this. It'll be okay," Victor whispered while rubbing circles into her back.

CREED
by *Phoenix Daniels*

Taylor clung to him, crying into his tuxedo. Victor held her until she began to calm.

"Come on, babe. Let's get you home."

"I can't leave," she said, shaking her head. "You go, and I'll call you if anything changes."

"No, we're gonna get you in some fresh clothes and come back. Kena has made arrangements with the hospital. They're providing us with a room for the night."

Taylor was amazed by his thoughtfulness. "Us?"

"Us," he confirmed.

"Wait, really? She can do that?" Taylor asked, looking up into beautiful green eyes that were filled with sympathy.

"Of course," he responded while using his thumb to wipe a tear from under her eye. "She's a very powerful woman."

"Thank you, Victor," she chuckled.

As she stared into his eyes, she was suddenly hit with such raw emotion. It was as if she had just been kicked in the gut. Just as she couldn't fathom life without Maria, life without Victor she simply couldn't bear.

She loved him.

Yeah, she loved him.

She turned to Kena. "Thanks, Kena."

CREED
by *Phoenix Daniels*

Kena rubbed Taylor's arm and gave her a reassuring nod, before disappearing down the hall. "Come on. Let's go."

"Victor, I gotta find out what happened first."

"Kenyatta will find out," he said, placing an insistent hand in the small of her back and ushering her through the path that Gregor and his team made in the crowded hallway.

Taylor was quiet on the ride to her house. Victor held her hand as he fielded phone calls from his office. She stared out of the window, wondering if Maria was in pain. Victor barely finished his call before his phone rang again.

"Kena, what do you have?"

The mention of Kena's name caused Taylor to turn to Victor. She waited, not so patiently, as she gave him an update. And just when she thought that she'd have an anxiety attack, Victor thanked Kena and ended the call.

"According to the report, due to a shortage of manpower, Maria was working alone. The dispatcher assigned another car to a burglary in process. Maria went to back them up. The report said that while Maria and the other officers on scene searched a building, that turned out to be abandoned, they heard shots fired. They said by the time they made it to Maria that she was already down. She was shot twice in the back."

"Oh, my God," Taylor gasped.

CREED
by *Phoenix Daniels*

Taylor allowed Victor to pull her on his lap. She placed her head on his shoulder and allowed tears to fall as he rocked her back and forward.

"Were there any arrests?" she whimpered.

"No arrests, no suspects. I'm sorry, baby."

Collier turned into Taylor's driveway. She slid off of Victor's lap and grabbed her purse. When they got out of the limo, Gregor escorted them to the front door. He suddenly held his hand out, halting their steps. The front door had been kicked in. Taylor snatched her off-duty 380 out of her purse and tossed her purse to the ground. She stepped around Gregor and entered her house before Victor could stop her. She knew that if she hadn't moved quickly, she would've had to fight to get away. She knew that he was just concerned, but this was what she did, and this was her home.

"Governor, I need to take you back to the limo," Gregor insisted, taking his own weapon out of its holster.

"Are you out of your fucking mind? I'm to send my woman in there alone?

Taylor looked back, just long enough to see Victor pulling his own weapon from the back of his pants. He ordered Gregor to move.

"Governor, I-" Gregor started.

CREED
by *Phoenix Daniels*

"Now!" he gritted.

She could still hear Victor and Gregor's argument outside, but she did her best to block them out so that she could hear any movement in the house. She walked along the wall with her weapon ready. Hearing soft footsteps behind her, she turned to see Victor and Gregor brandishing weapons of their own. She turned back and continued along the wall. She saw movement outside of her kitchen window and recognized someone from Victor's security detail, so she continued her search.

Ten minutes later, after a complete search of the house that turned up nothing, Taylor dialed 911. She reported the break-in to the operator and was instructed to wait for the police.

"Victor, what were you thinking?" Taylor asked, walking over to the refrigerator.

She was desperate for a glass of wine or a shot of something.

"Taylor, what the hell were you thinking, running your ass in the house?" His irritation was evident.

"Victor, this is what I do for a living. But you're the gotdamn governor of Illinois. You can't do shit like this," she said, equally frustrated.

"You're not at work. When you're with me, you're not a cop. You're my woman. So, if you don't want me running behind you, don't run your lone ranger ass into dangerous situations."

CREED
by *Phoenix Daniels*

"So what if something had happened to you? How the hell am I supposed to handle that? How the hell would Gregor explain you dying on his watch?"

Victor tilted his head and looked at her like she had lost her mind. "Gregor?! He'd find employment at a fucking ice cream shop! This is a job to him; I die, he gets another. So you tell me; how the hell am I supposed to live with myself if I was sitting my ass in a limo and you got hurt, or worse?"

Taylor responded with a shake of her head. She wasn't going to win the argument, and she wasn't in the mood to fight with him. There was already too much going on. She opened the fridge, but instead of pulling out a bottle of wine, she pulled out a note instead.

It simply read: ***WATCH YOUR BACK IN DARK PLACES!***

CREED
by *Phoenix Daniels*

CHAPTER 22
Taylor

Taylor drew a sharp breath and dropped the note as if it were burning her hand. She watched it drift slowly to the floor. A sharp pain penetrated her skull, and her racing heart was beating loudly in her ear. Taylor braced herself against the refrigerator door, inhaling and exhaling slowly, trying to calm her raging heart.

It was a cop!

A cop shot Maria!

A cop had just threatened her!

A cop!

With her eyes blinded by angry tears, Taylor could barely see Victor hurrying to her. She felt his hands on her upper arms and faintly heard his voice.

"What, baby? What is it?" she heard through the haze.

Unable to find her voice, Taylor pointed to the note on the floor. Victor walked her over to the breakfast bar and urged her to sit on a stool. She wiped her face as Victor picked the note up and read it. As he read, his expression changed—it was beyond murderous. He placed the note on the counter and walked over to Taylor. Staring directly into her eyes, he said, "Whoever did this has fucked up. Now they have to deal with me."

She nodded in the affirmative because Victor was right about one thing: *they had fucked up,* because Taylor planned to put a bullet into the head of the bastard that put those bullets into Maria. They could come for her if they wanted to, but they would be leaving with some hot shit in their ass!

CREED
by *Phoenix Daniels*

Kena's knock at the door interrupted Taylor's heinous thoughts. When Kena walked in wearing a troubled expression, Taylor became uneasy.

"Is it Maria?" Taylor asked, hopping down off of the stool.

"No, there's no change. The doctor said that they were giving her blood in order to raise her blood pressure for surgery."

"Then what is it, Kenyatta?" Victor asked.

Kena placed a newspaper on the breakfast bar. The headline read:

GOVERNOR'S GIRL INVOLVED IN POLICE SHOOTING OF UNARMED MAN!
PROTESTORS GATHER AT THE THOMPSON CENTER!

The article, written by Brent Trainer, described the blatant murder of an unarmed Black man by the police and the attempt to cover it up. It went on to mention that Taylor was the officer involved in a foot chase with said unarmed Black man. It never once included the fact that Taylor wasn't the officer that had actually shot him.

Taylor laughed out loud, causing Victor and Kena to look at her curiously. They must have thought she was losing her mind because there clearly wasn't anything humorous about the newspaper article. Taylor wasn't amused; she was exhausted to the point of hysteria. But she was under attack, and she didn't have time for a breakdown. To hell with the media. To hell with the department. Taylor's one and only focus was finding the bastard that shot her friend.

"I need to get back to the hospital. I'm gonna go change," Taylor announced calmly.

She could feel their eyes burning into her as she left the room. And she was sure that Victor was having an inner debate with himself on whether or not to follow. But, gratefully, he stayed put, giving her the alone time that she needed.

CREED

by *Phoenix Daniels*

CREED

Victor looked at the newspaper again, unable to believe the unmitigated gall of that pussy, Brent Trainer. Victor was a man with power, but shutting down the media wasn't something even a governor could do. He *was* tempted to put a hit out on Brent's ass.

"Renee Griffin called," Kena announced. "She says that she's already ahead of this article."

"Good. Tell Gregor to put together a team for Taylor. Tell him to keep it covert, because if Taylor finds out, she'll have a fit."

"Governor, that's just not safe. You want them to follow an angry woman that carries a gun… without her knowledge?"

"Yeah, so tell them not to get shot."

Kena gaped at him in disbelief, seconds before muttering, "Yes, sir."

Taylor came out of her bedroom just as calm as when she went in. Kena watched her with concern, trying to gauge her demeanor, but Victor didn't need to study her demeanor at all. As soon as she saw that headline, he recognized the need for vengeance in her eyes. She was formulating a plan: retaliation.

"You okay, babe?" Victor asked.

"I'm good," Taylor responded without emotion. "I'm not waiting for the evidence technician. They ain't gonna find shit anyway. Can we go?"

"Yes. Kena has someone coming by to fix your door. She's gonna grab enough of your personal effects for you to stay at the penthouse. You're moving in with me."

CREED
by *Phoenix Daniels*

Taylor's brows bunched and her arms instantly crossed over her chest. Victor was ready for this; he had already known that she was going to put up a fight.

"Is that right?" she asked with narrowed eyes.

"Yes, ma'am, that's right."

"Victor, nobody is gonna make me leave my own home," she declared. "This..." she said, waving her hand, "....is *my* house."

Victor stepped into her personal space, but Taylor refused to cower. She raised her chin, defiantly, and stood her ground. Victor almost smiled, but he resisted.

"Babe, this is not going to be a fight. You're in danger. You'll stay with me."

"I'm not gonna tuck my tail and run," Taylor rebutted with a shake of her head. "*This* is my house and ain't *nobody* gonna run me out of it."

Victor needed to make her understand that she was his responsibility. She was his—his love.

Damn!

He was in love with her already!

She couldn't have realized that she consumed his every thought. Thoughts of her were the only thing that brought a smile to his face. He would give his own life to give her peace. That had to be love, right?

Sadly, though he loved her, the fact that she was now tethered to him thrust her into the media's spotlight.

"Sweetness, it's just for a little while. You've been threatened. You're in danger."

CREED
by *Phoenix Daniels*

"I don't care, Victor. I'm not running. My job comes with danger," she responded as if she expected to have the last word.

Victor grabbed her face. He needed her to understand how serious he was. Taylor was stubborn, and that was okay. He liked that about her, but there were times when he would have to take the lead.

"Taylor, I wouldn't give a fuck if you were Walker Texas Fucking Ranger! To be honest, I don't give a shit about your career. I'm sorry, but I don't. You belong to me! Do you hear me? Me!"

Taylor blinked up at him, but she didn't respond. Victor was thankful that he didn't have to shut down any more rebuttals, so he continued.

"You're not a fucking cop; not right now. You are my, Victor Creed the II's, lady. Mine! With that being said, it is no longer your job to protect you; it's mine. "

Victor made his declaration, not knowing what to expect. But he meant every word. To his relief, Taylor relented. She wrapped her arms around his neck and kissed his chin.

"I love you, Victor," she whispered, to his amazement.

Victor's smile would've been considered too giddy for a grown ass man. "You do?"

"I do," she confirmed, to his delight.

"Good, because I love you too, Sweetness."

CREED
by *Phoenix Daniels*

CHAPTER 23

TAYLOR

Taylor moved a file and slipped into bed next to Victor. They were in a fancy room that seemed more like a hotel room than a hospital room. It was a little after three in the morning. Maria had pulled through surgery and was placed in a medically induced coma while she healed. Thankfully, she was expected to make a full recovery.

Victor was sitting with his back to the headboard working on his laptop. Papers were spread all over the bed. Taylor watched silently as Victor worked, unable to quell the guilt that she was beginning to feel. Victor was a busy man with an entire state to run, yet he hadn't left Taylor's side to do so.

"Victor?" she cooed, breaking the silence.

"Yeah, babe?"

"Have I told you how awesome you are?"

Victor removed his reading glasses and looked over at Taylor. He grinned, showing off those adorable dimples that she loved so much.

"No, but I'm listening," he said in a husky voice.

Taylor studied his features, fascinated how a man with pretty green eyes, long dark lashes, and dimples could still be so damn masculine. Taylor, instead of telling him, decided to show him just how awesome he was. She was going to let her bad girl takeover.

She rose to her knees and looked him square in the eye. His dark, olive gaze glimmered with the possibility of carnality.

CREED

by *Phoenix Daniels*

Without breaking eye contact, she slowly began to remove all of the work-related items from the bed, placing them on the nightstand. Once the bed was cleared, she straddled his lap and pulled his t-shirt over his head. She pushed her fingers through his hair and guided his face to her own. Covering his lips with her own, she expressed the passion that she felt for him through her kiss. His hands flew to her hips, and he pulled her forward, forcing her to grind her warm, eager core against his fully erect dick. The size of his manhood was an unbearable temptation, but pleasing herself wasn't what Taylor had in mind. Taylor's plan was to make it all about Victor.

"Baby," she purred. "I know how much you love to please."

"I do," Victor growled.

"I know, but I gotta put my foot down."

"Yeah?"

"Yeah, baby," Taylor said, licking her lips.

"Okay, sweetness, do your thing."

He had a mischievous gleam in his eye as he moved to lie down. Taylor took that as a go and pulled his boxers down. His big, solid dick sprang free and welcomed her. She wrapped her fingers around the velvety shaft and took him into her mouth. She slid him in and out, making sure to saturate him well. Once completely lubricated, Victor grabbed a handful of her kinky curls and guided his dick in and out of her hot, wet mouth. He let out a loud moan as she took as much of him as she could. Taylor gripped him tight and stroked his velvety shaft hard. He raised his hips, pushing between her eager, hungry lips. Taylor found herself moaning at the sheer satisfaction of giving him pleasure. She tightened her lips

CREED
by *Phoenix Daniels*

around the head of his throbbing dick and sucked him the way that he deserved to be sucked. Taylor poured every ounce of her gratitude into the blowjob that she was giving. His fingers tightened in her hair, and his moans became louder.

"Oooh, yesss! Fuck me with that hot fucking mouth of yours," he commanded forcefully.

As she orally worked him, Taylor stared deep into his hooded eyes, eliciting a feral growl. His hips rose frantically from the bed, and he fucked her mouth as if it were her hot pussy.

"Fuuuuuuck, Tay... Baby, I'm cumming!" he shouted. "Harder!"

Taylor obliged. She sucked him and stroked him in a maniacal manner. She moaned around his dick and reached up to massage his balls, taking him completely over the edge. He instantly began to shoot hot semen into her mouth.

Victor sank into the mattress and groaned as Taylor swallowed and sucked him clean. She looked up at him and licked her lips, hoping that she had accomplished her goal of proving just how wonderful he was. He had earned every stroke, every lick, and every hot and hungry suck of his big, thick dick. And if it had taken all night, she would have sucked him all night.

"Damn... Just... damn," he panted while rubbing her hair.

CHAPTER 24

CREED

Victor watched Taylor closely as she packed their overnight bags. He was assessing her mood for the conversation to come. Taylor was a very, almost overly, independent woman, who sometimes didn't listen to reason.

"Babe?"

"Yes?"

"Have you considered taking some time off work?" he asked, tentatively.

Taylor stopped what she was doing and looked at him with narrowed eyes. "Victor, no."

Her response was more like a warning for him not to go there. Taylor seriously thought she was running the show. He was almost amused. She clearly didn't realize that he could have her benched with one phone call. Of course, he wouldn't do that without reason, but if he didn't think that he could keep her safe, he definitely would.

"Taylor, I just got a call from Kena. Apparently, protesters are popping up all over the city. With your face being on the front page of the Times, I'm not feeling good about you going back on the street."

Taylor exhaled and walked over to him. She sat on his lap and ran her fingers through his thick hair.

"Baby, please, I need you to trust that I can take care of myself," she implored.

CREED
by *Phoenix Daniels*

"I do trust that you can take care of yourself, Taylor, but you're only one person. You see what happened to Maria. Those cops are either gonna fail to back you up on the street or shoot you themselves."

Taylor didn't respond. Instead, she began to chew on her bottom lip. Before Victor could ask her what she was thinking, she said, in a soft voice, "You're right, baby. I'll take some time off."

Victor, unable to hide his shock, had expected her to put up more of a fight. "Really?"

"Yeah, really," she said in a tone that was a little too upbeat and bubbly.

She gave him a quick peck before hopping off of his lap and walking across the hospital room to finish packing their things.

Too easy, Victor thought.

She was up to something. Victor could practically see the formulation of a plan in her head. She thought she was pulling one over on him. Little did she know, she was going to have a twenty-four-hour tail. Therefore, he would know exactly what it was that she had up her sleeve.

CREED

by *Phoenix Daniels*

TAYLOR

Victor dropped Taylor at his apartment and continued on to his office. As soon as she walked into his penthouse, she dropped her bag by the door and headed right back out. She pulled out her phone and activated the Uber application. She needed to get to her house and pick up her car. The app indicated that the driver was six minutes away, so she used that time to make some calls. She fished through her contacts until she found the number that she was looking for. Once she reached the lobby, she made her call.

"Detective Deveraux," the voice announced on the other end.

"Bella, It's Taylor. I need your help."

"Tay? What's up? I heard about Maria. How is she?"

Taylor could hear genuine concern in her voice.

"She's gonna be fine."

Bella breathed a sigh of relief. "That's good. What do need?"

"I need to see everything they got on Maria's shooting."

"Well... it's not my case, but I'll pull everything I can."

"Bella, I need to see every witness statement. I need to know every cop that was on the scene. And I need to see whatever forensics reports that were generated."

"Taylor, you're thinking this was a cop, aren't you?"

"Wow, you're the best detective ever," Taylor scoffed.

"You want me to help your ass or not?"

"Okay, I'm sorry," Taylor chuckled.

CREED

by *Phoenix Daniels*

"Taylor, I know you and Maria ain't exactly on those good ole boys' Christmas lists, but do you really think they'd go this far?"

"Jim Gore is getting charged with murder. Maria and I are the prosecution's star witnesses. Hell yeah, they'll go that far."

"Yeah, it's something to think about. I'll do what I can."

"Thanks a bunch. Can you meet at the scene in an hour?"

"Yeah, no problem. But listen, if it was a cop that shot Maria, you need to be very careful."

Before Taylor could respond, a red Camry pulled in front of the building.

"My Uber's here. I'll see you in a bit."

"Uber?... Never mind, I don't wanna know," Bella chuckled.

Twenty minutes later, Taylor was standing in her garage, deciding between her Mustang or her bike. With her decision made, Taylor grabbed her nine millimeter out of her purse and stuffed it into the back of her pants. She pulled her shirt over it and placed her purse in the seat compartment. She hopped on and walked it out of the garage. After closing the garage door, she was off.

Taylor kicked into high gear, thinking that if her new bodyguards wanted to babysit her, they'd have to keep up with her Monster. Taylor may have been a lot of things, but a fool wasn't one of them. She knew that she was being tailed, and she'd bet money that it was Victor that placed the tail on her. His intentions were good, but a security detail would only get in her way.

CREED
by *Phoenix Daniels*

She weaved in and out of traffic in a way that a car never could. By the time she pulled in front of the building where Maria was shot, she was certain that she had shaken anyone that was following her. She climbed off of the bike and walked over to the front of the building, just as a department-issued old school Chevy Caprice was pulling behind her bike. Belladonna Deveraux stepped out, looking like anything but the tough CPD detective that she was. She was a tall African American with strong Native American features. Her long and straight jet black hair, sharp nose and dark feline-shaped eyes were an obvious clue of her genealogy. She was wearing a simple white t-shirt, skinny jeans, and sneaker wedges.

"Girl, you hopped out that hoopty looking more like a supermodel than a cop," Taylor chuckled. "Yo' pretty ass gotta be beating guys off with a stick."

"Girl, bye," Bella scoffed. "These looks ain't never got me nothing but face down and ass up. But, on the other hand, you be proppin' all that ass up on that bike. If you ever look back, I'll bet there's a line of thirsty ass dudes tailing you."

Taylor laughed and embraced her friend. Bella and Taylor were partners for years before Bella got promoted to detective, leaving Taylor behind. At the time of the detective's exam, Taylor hadn't had enough time on the job, rendering her ineligible to even take the test. When Bella was transferred to the detective division, Taylor was sad to lose her partner. Bella was kind and thoughtful, and Taylor often wondered why her parents would name her after a deadly poison.

"So, you're banging our sexy ass governor, huh? He packin'?" she chortled.

"Subtle," Taylor muttered. "So subtle."

CREED
by *Phoenix Daniels*

"Well?" Bella prodded.

"The entire state of Illinois knows that I'm involved with Victor, and what he's packing ain't none of your business. Don't make me cut yo' ass," Taylor half-joked.

"Okay, okay, fair enough," Bella said, raising her hands in surrender. "Come on. Let me show you what I got."

They walked toward the entrance of the building. The front door was boarded, and there was crime scene tape sealing it off from the public. Since the evidence techs had already processed the scene, Taylor had no problem ripping the tape and entering. They stepped into a small foyer that led to a set of stairs that looked less than stable. Bella shined a light in the dark, dusty building.

"Okay, first off, if someone breaks into an abandoned building, where there's clearly nothing to steal, how would a citizen call that in?" Bella asked.

Taylor contemplated for a few seconds before responding. "They would call it in as a burglary."

"And how do we as cops classify this?"

"As... criminal trespassing."

"Exactly, so listen to this…"

Bella pulled out a small recorder and pushed play. It was a copy of the 911 call. After listening to the caller, Taylor knew immediately where Bella was going. Her face burned with anger as she continued to listen to the recording. Once the call ended, Bella turned off the recording and asked, "What did you hear?"

"I heard a caller telling the 911 call-taker that there was a criminal trespass in progress. The bitch actually said in progress," Taylor seethed.

CREED
by *Phoenix Daniels*

"That ain't all you heard. Describe the voice."

"Umm... female, maybe middle-aged, and, if I had to guess, white."

"Yeah, and where the fuck are we?"

"Roseland," Taylor replied with a nod.

Taylor was reading Bella loud and clear. Roseland wasn't occupied by many white families. So what were the chances of a white bystander, that just so happened to sound like a cop, hanging out in a majority black neighborhood long enough to observe a burglary and report it as a criminal trespass in progress? The odds weren't impossible, but very slim.

"Aaand," Bella added. "I took a drive around the back. The windows are barred, and the back door is cemented. Whoever shot Maria was either already inside, or came in with her. She was shot in the back on her way up those stairs."

After searching the building for anything that the techs might have left behind, they exited the building.

"Even though it was a female caller, I'm still looking into Gore and his rookie partner's whereabouts that night," Bella told Taylor. "But... ain't no tellin' how many cops have jumped on their bandwagon. I'll let you know what I find out."

"Thanks, Bella. It's hard to know who to trust on this job, so I appreciate you for helping me out."

"Anytime, girl. You know that," she said over her shoulder as she walked to her car.

Taylor nodded and smiled because she actually did know that. Other than Maria, Bella was her closest friend in the department.

Taylor slipped her helmet over her head and climbed on her bike. She pulled off behind Bella. Once they made it to the

CREED
by *Phoenix Daniels*

expressway, Taylor passed Bella and honked. Bella honked once in return.

Taylor was riding at a moderate speed, going over everything that she'd just learned. Sadly, even with all the information that Bella was able to get, all of it was speculative. Proving that Gore, or anyone else in the department, had something to do with the shooting wasn't going to be an easy task. But it was a task that Taylor was taking to heart. The shooting of an unarmed man, Maria getting shot, and the threats made to her, showed Taylor just how little human life meant to some.

Taylor, so engulfed in her thoughts, almost hadn't noticed the dark SUV that was moving dangerously fast behind her. She immediately changed lanes to see if the driver was simply in a hurry. But once the SUV was parallel to her, she was face-to-face with the business end of a firearm. She gripped the clutch and kicked it up to the sixth gear, riding faster than she'd ever ridden, successfully leaving the SUV in the dust. But, all of a sudden, a dark sedan swerved into the same lane, almost clipping her rear tire. When the sedan sped to parallel her right side, Taylor snatched her pistol from the back of her pants. When the barrel of a shotgun extended out of the back window, Taylor fired a succession of shots at the driver. The sedan began to swerve and veer to the side. She must have hit the driver.

Good.

Unfortunately, Taylor's brief celebration was short-lived when she was suddenly, struck from behind and sent flying to the grassy knoll on the side of the expressway. Unable to control the bike, Taylor dropped... *hard.*

CREED

by *Phoenix Daniels*

She hit the ground screaming, knowing immediately that her shoulder was either broken or badly dislocated. Her vision was blurred by tears, but she knew that she needed to run. Still, no matter how hard she tried, she couldn't move. She could faintly hear cries of agony and suddenly realized that they were her own. Taylor had never felt such intense pain in her life, and she didn't think it could get any worse until she was mercilessly flipped onto her back. She howled in agony as her helmet was yanked from her head. Whoever wanted her dead was about to get their wish. Taylor was sure of it. And although she cried, she refused to beg. She took a painful breath and looked directly into the eye of the person that was about to end her life. Her heart nearly stopped when she saw the face hovering above her. To say that she was shocked was a gross understatement. Warm tears escaped her eyes, falling into her ears.

"W-why?" she choked.

Without the mercy of an explanation, he pointed his weapon and fired a shot into Taylor's chest. Her body jerked violently upon impact. As she began to lose consciousness, she realized that a bullet had actually entered her body, and although it burned, it wasn't as painful as she would have assumed. As she looked up at the angry, but familiar face, thoughts of the people she loved danced around in her mind. But just before the world went dark, it was his name that she cried out.

CREED
by *Phoenix Daniels*

CHAPTER 25

CREED

"What do you mean you lost her?" Victor questioned, leaning back in his chair.

"Sir, she was on a motorcycle," Gregor explained, apologetically.

Victor tossed his reading glasses on his desk and rubbed his brow in frustration. That damn bike; it made Taylor look even sexier than Victor thought possible, and it was going to be a problem. He knew that he wasn't overreacting or being too overprotective. Something inside of Victor warned him that Taylor was in real danger, and she wasn't taking the threat seriously enough for him. Then it dawned on him; Taylor might have spotted her tail and slipped them on purpose.

"Find her," Victor demanded.

"I'm working on it, sir."

"Governor Creed, Renee Griffin is here to see you," Lisa announced.

"Send her in," he replied. Then he told Gregor, "Thanks. Let me know as soon as you find her."

"Yes, sir."

Gregor opened the door to Victor's office and stepped to the side, allowing Renee to enter. Renee took one look at Victor and asked, "Is everything okay?"

Victor forced a smile, appreciating her concern.

"Yes. Whatcha got?"

CREED
by *Phoenix Daniels*

Renee placed the Times on his desk. The headline read:
GOVERNOR'S GIRL NOT THE SHOOTER!

Victor read the article that detailed how Taylor wasn't the cop that shot the unarmed car thief. It went on to describe Taylor and Maria as the fearless cops that defied the police department and their fellow officers by telling the truth.

"This is good work, Miss Griffin."

"Thank you, sir."

"Why didn't I hire you to begin with?"

"Hell if I know," she scoffed, causing Victor to laugh.

It was the first time that Renee was anything but formal with him. She was beginning to relax. But before Victor could relax into a comfortable banter with her, a news headline flashed across the bottom of the muted television screen:
GOVERNOR'S GIRLFRIEND MURDERED: GUNNED DOWN ON INTERSTATE 94.

Victor jumped from his chair, only to fall back into his seat. He gasped, struggling to catch his breath. He'd just had the wind knocked out of him, and his heart nearly stopped. Surely this was just another bullshit media headline. Taylor hadn't been gunned down. He had almost successfully convinced himself until Kena tore into his office in tears.

CREED

by *Phoenix Daniels*

CHAPTER 26

CREED

Victor ran from his town car through the emergency room doors, not giving a damn about the rapid flashes of the cameras pointed at him. He stopped at a counter, just long enough to shout, "Taylor Montgomery!"

"Governor Creed!" He heard from a voice behind.

Victor stared pointedly at the nurse in front of him, ignoring the voice.

"Governor!" The voice insisted with more force.

Victor turned around, locating the woman that was interrupting his progress. He needed to see Taylor. He shot daggers at the woman and yelled, "What?!'

The woman had a gun attached to her hip, looking like she was ready to go toe to toe with his security detail. She must have been a cop. His security detail was blocking her path.

"Let her through," he ordered.

She shook the men off and walked over to him.

"Governor Creed, my name is Bella Deveraux. I'm a detective with the Chicago Police Department."

She wasn't winning any points with Victor by the announcement, and she could tell, because she quickly added, "I'm also a close friend of Taylor's."

"Okay?"

"I saw the news and Taylor's not dead. She took a bullet to the chest, but she's very much alive. She's in surgery."

Victor exhaled. He'd never been so relieved in his entire life. The thought of losing Taylor was the worst possible scenario in his life; and his wife had died. Truthfully, he'd never felt such loss when he thought that Taylor was gone. Contrary

CREED

by *Phoenix Daniels*

to Rosemary, he was in love with Taylor. He did loved Rosemary, but he was never in love with her.

"Sir, I can take you to where the rest of her family is waiting," Bella offered.

"Okay, yes, thank you."

"This way."

Victor followed the detective down the hall with his security detail in tow. She led him to a private waiting room where James, her dad, an elegant older woman, and the sister that he'd met at the State Dinner were waiting. Every one of them seemed positively distraught. Victor wondered how he was the last to know. After all, he'd placed a fucking tail on her.

James walked over and placed his hand on Victor's shoulder.

"Listen here, boy, my small fry is gone pull through this. You hear me?"

"Yes, sir, I hear you," Victor agreed with tears forming in his eyes. "She has to, sir."

"She will," James assured. "This is my wife, Martha."

Victor looked into the eyes of Taylor's mom, unable to stop his own tears. Normally, he was a man that exercised control in all things, but he couldn't control the fear of losing the woman he loved. Martha pulled him into her arms and embraced him as only a mother could. Victor inhaled her sweet scent as she held him tight.

"Um mm," she said as she rocked him.

"Our girl ain't goin' nowhere."

"I know," Victor whispered.

"Come on and sit down."

She led him to a chair and urged him into the seat. There, she held his hand until a doctor with a surgical mask resting under his chin entered the waiting room.

"It was touch and go, but she's gonna make it," he announced with pride, staring directly at Victor.

CREED
by *Phoenix Daniels*

Breathing a sigh of relief, Victor thanked God. But, it was clear that the doctor was basking in the glory of saving the governor's girlfriend. Victor stood and looked the ambitious surgeon directly in the eye.

"Repeat that, but this time say it to her mother."

The young surgeon lowered his head before doing as instructed.

Taylor's family was thanking God as Victor looked to the detective, Bella Deveraux.

"What happened?" He asked.

"She asked me to meet her where Maria was shot. She wanted details about Maria's shooting, but she didn't trust anyone in the department," she said with a glare, ensuring that he understood her implication.

"I get it. Go on," Victor urged.

"Well, I gave her some info that may have indicated that it was a cop that shot Maria. When we left, Taylor took off on her bike. I was a little ways behind her. A few minutes later, I see her in a full out fucking gun battle on the E-way. I tried to get to her as fast as I could, but by the time I made it to her, she'd been run off the road. I immediately pulled over, and tried to get to her as fast as I could... I swear I did. But, when I got there, that motherfucker had already put a bullet in her chest. And he was about to shoot her again until I put three into him."

"Who?" Victor asked. "Who was it?"

Bella reached into her back pocket and pulled out a piece of paper.

"His name was Collier, Collier Sanders."

Victor's eyes widened. Surely, the detective was mistaken. Collier?! Why the fuck would Collier shoot Taylor? Bella noticed Victor's reaction, her eyes narrowed as she asked, "Governor Creed, do you know this Collier?"

"Yeah, he's my driver," Victor admitted, still confused. "But why would Collier shoot Taylor?"

CREED
by *Phoenix Daniels*

"I don't know," Bella told him. "Before he passed out, he said that it wasn't his idea, that *she* made him do it."

"And who is she?" Victor asked.

"I don't know," Bella responded, shaking her head. "But, believe that I plan to find out exactly who *she* is."

"Is he dead," Victor asked, saying a short prayer in his mind.

"Naw, he's in surgery."

The detective appeared to be disappointed, but Victor smiled inwardly, because God had answered his prayers.

CREED

by *Phoenix Daniels*

TAYLOR

Taylor could hear faded voices that seemed to be coming from far away. It was as if she was wearing earmuffs or plugs. She felt like she was floating underwater. It was only when she heard his voice that Taylor struggled to reach the surface.

"Taylor, baby, can you open your eyes?"

It was Victor.

Taylor struggled to open her eyes. As her lashes fluttered, she was grateful for the first flash of light. Well, she *was* grateful, until the first stab of pain hit her chest; a pain so fierce it was as if God himself was standing on her chest. Taylor squeezed her eyes shut and gasped for air.

"Victor," escaped her lips in a panic.

She didn't know how she'd gathered the strength or the courage to speak. She could feel his hand caressing her face and hear his soothing voice, encouraging her to relax and breathe. Needing to see the beauty in his eyes, Taylor made another attempt at opening hers. When they fluttered this time, she was greeted by beautiful moss colored irises that were framed by luscious dark lashes.

"Hi, baby. I missed you," he whispered softly in a deep masculine voice.

"I-I..." Taylor coughed. She cleared her throat, which was a most painful mistake. Taylor's memories of being shot flooded her mind. "I love you, Victor," she whispered carefully.

"I know, sweetness. I love you too."

"How bad is it? Am I going to live?"

CREED
by *Phoenix Daniels*

"Do you think that I would allow another alternative?"

Taylor would've chuckled if she weren't positive that it would cause her great pain. "No," she whispered hoarsely.

Victor massaged her hairline while planting kisses against her temple, easing her pain with his touch. Of course, not all of her pain, but enough so that she could look into his eyes, smile, and attempt to reassure him that she was okay.

"Your family is waiting to see you. I pulled some strings to get in here first."

"Of course, you did," Taylor mused.

She took careful, shallow breaths to avoid the massive pain that breathing caused. "Victor..."

"No, baby, don't talk. Rest," he insisted.

"Okay, but, it was Collier. Collier sho-," she wheezed.

"Shhh..." Victor interrupted. "I know. It's okay. I'll take care of it."

"Victor, wait..." Taylor winced as she reached for him.

"Taylor, baby, please relax. You have to stay calm. Don't worry about Collier or anyone else. I'll take care of it."

CREED

"Governor, I cleared as much of your week as I could. And I-" Kena froze mid-sentence and clutched her imaginary pearls. Her breath hitched, and her skin was flushed. Victor turned to see what had affected her so obviously. It was the four large, imposing men entering the main entrance. The Creed brothers took long intent strides toward him. And although they weren't smiling, Victor grinned at not only Kena's reaction but every other woman's reaction to their presence. His baby brothers had a tendency to command a room.

All of his brothers had thick, dark hair like Victor Sr. But only two of them had his green eyes. The youngest two had their mother's blue eyes. They were tall and bulky as him, except for Jaysen, the baby. He was taller than them all but athletically lean.

Victor found comfort in his brothers' presence, as they took turns embracing him.

"How's your lady?" Lucas, the second born, asked.

"She's stable and awake," Victor exhaled.

"Good," Lincoln chimed. "Where can we talk?"

It was just like Lincoln Creed to be all business. It was the Army Ranger in him. He didn't engage in much small talk. Lincoln was known for getting right to the point, but since they were in mixed company, he couldn't. It wasn't the time for the kind of talk that they needed to have.

"Jaysen, Alex, Lucas, you've already met Kenyatta, my assistant," Victor said, gesturing to Kena, who was still frozen next to him.

CREED
by *Phoenix Daniels*

His brothers nodded with smiles as they acknowledged her.

"Kena, meet my brother, Lincoln."

Lincoln seemed to notice Kena for the first time. His serious expression completely changed. He was no longer all business, as his eyes roamed her from head to toe. He stepped close enough to violate Kena's personal space and smiled down at her. She seemed to stop breathing altogether, and Victor worried that she might pass out.

"Kena, do you think you can arrange a private room where we can talk?" Victor intervened.

"Oh… yeah. *Yes*, sir, I'm on it," Kena blinked, regaining her composure.

She reluctantly turned to step away, but Lincoln captured her hand and brought it to his lips, saying, "It was a pleasure to meet you, Kenyatta. I can't wait to see you again." Lincoln was pouring on the charm.

Kara smiled nervously. "It was nice to meet you, Mr. Creed."

"Linc," he insisted.

She pulled her hand free, but it was too late. Victor could already see the slight buckling of her knees. Kena stumbled away without looking back.

"Linc, don't fuck with my assistant's head. After Taylor and Mom, she's the most important woman in my life."

"I'm not gonna fuck her *head*," Linc said with a smirk.

His brothers chuckled, but Victor wasn't amused. He wasn't about to allow his brother to corrupt his assistant. "Lincoln, I'm serious. She's the most efficient woman in my life. She keeps me together."

CREED

by *Phoenix Daniels*

"Victor, mind your own business," Alex chimed. "You can't control what that woman does when she's not at work."

"The fuck I can't! Don't fuck with my assistant!" Victor blurted, causing his brothers to laugh.

"You hittin' that?" Lucas asked, leaning into Victor.

"Of course not!"

"Then shut the fuck up!"

"Fuck you, Luc! Don't make me kick your ass!"

Victor and his brothers were immediately silenced by the sound of their mother's voice. "Boys! Don't make me put you all in time out. If you're going to act like little boys, I'll have to treat you like little boys."

CREED
by *Phoenix Daniels*

CHAPTER 27

TAYLOR

The last thing she remembered was her family's visit. They were all smiling, feigning optimism, pretending as if nothing had happened. But Taylor understood that there was a hole in her chest created by a man's bullet. She also knew that her family, who had never wanted her to be a cop in the first place, was not optimistic. They were simply trying to be positive so that she would stay positive, and she loved them for it. But she was worn out, and the pain meds had her discombobulated, so she wasn't very disappointed when they left.

Finally, she opened her eyes from a much-needed slumber, but all she saw was blackness.

"I'm here, darling," came from a voice that was unfamiliar.

Taylor did her best not to panic. Panic would hurt.

"Who are you?" Taylor croaked.

"Tabatha, Tabatha Creed. I'm Victor's mother. I'm here to keep you company. How are you feeling? Are you in pain?"

Taylor exhaled, instantly relieved. "No, ma'am, I'm feeling okay. Thank you."

As the woman came closer, Taylor was able to see the beautiful redhead with vivid blue eyes that seemed to sparkle. She had a smile that was somehow calming.

She spoke softly with amusement in her eyes. "Don't lie to me, young lady. I'm a mother. I can always tell."

CREED
by *Phoenix Daniels*

"Well, I *could* use a little something for the pain," Taylor admitted.

Tabatha grabbed Taylor's chart from the footboard and studied it as if she knew what she was reading.

"Hmm... No allergies. I think you can have a little bit of Percocet. I'll talk with your doctor. He's been giving you Morphine. I think it's time to switch meds. Morphine can go really wrong when taken too long."

"Are you a doctor, Mrs. Creed?"

"Victor didn't tell you? That surprises me. Yes, I'm a cardiologist."

"No, ma'am. Victor always made you out to be 'Super-Housewife'. I thought you were a stay at home mom."

"Really?" Tabitha chuckled. "That's good to know. I always thought of myself as an absentee parent. It's good to know that he and his brothers didn't feel neglected."

Tabitha returned the chart to the foot of the bed and walked over to Taylor's side. She rubbed Taylor's wild hair out of her face and smiled down at her.

"Women...we work so hard to do it all, don't we?"

"Yes, ma'am," Taylor agreed with a weak smile.

"Look at you," Tabatha started. "You're this hardcore lady cop, but you're dating a high-profile man like Victor. You're accustomed to being in charge. But now, he's the one with the power. This is a major adjustment... no?"

"It is," Taylor admitted.

"I do understand. When I married Victor's father, I was the head of cardiology at the University of Chicago, and he was the junior senator of Indiana. It was hard for me to concede power and control, but he wouldn't have it any other way."

CREED
by *Phoenix Daniels*

Tabitha looked to the ceiling, remembering a time in her life. "Darling, that Victor… I mean, *my* Victor, Victor Sr., is all man," she commented, damn near swooning.

Taylor could see that Victor Sr. was still making Tabitha weak in the knees. She seemed very much in love. And why not? Even in his advanced years, the man was fine.

"So, Mrs. Creed, did you give up your career for love?"

"Hell no, are you crazy?" Tabitha said with a chuckle. "Why in the hell would I do that? Go through all those years of school, fight my way to the top, just to give it up to be the wife of a senator? No."

Taylor liked her gumption and was enjoying their conversation. But in the middle of it, the pain hit. "Mrs. Creed?" she groaned.

"Oh, please. Call me Tabitha, or Tabby. I like Tabby."

"Okay, Miss Tabby, can you make that Percocet happen?"

"Of course, darling," Tabatha chuckled. "Give me a few minutes."

CREED

by *Phoenix Daniels*

CREED

Victor and his brothers sat in the small hospital conference room, trying to figure out how to get to Collier. He was recovering from several gunshot wounds a few doors away from Taylor. His room was highly guarded by the State Police. Since Taylor was a Chicago Police Officer, CPD wasn't trusted with the task of keeping him alive.

"I can get to him," Lincoln Creed assured his brothers.

"Yeah, Linc, we know you can get to him, but we need to get to him without causing a national incident," Lucas chimed in. "That motherfucker has more security right now than Victor."

"He does," Victor said, nodding in agreement. "Linc, even if you could get in and get out without being detected, we still need to exercise a little patience. He's goin' nowhere. Besides, right now, I just wanna make sure that Taylor is going to be okay."

"I agree with Luc and Victor," Jaysen added. "If that asshole were to come up missing now, they'd look right at Victor. We gotta be smart about this."

"Okay, so what's the plan?" Lincoln asked.

"Hold tight until I say when," Victor instructed.

His brothers nodded their compliance, reminding him of when they were younger. No matter how old, big, or strong his little brothers got, they followed Victor's lead. Not that they weren't strong and powerful in their own rights. To others, his brothers would have been considered masters of the universe. But to Victor, they would always be his baby brothers.

CREED
by *Phoenix Daniels*

A knock at the door interrupted Victor's nostalgic moment. Kena peeked into the doorway. "Governor, Detective Deveraux would like to speak with you,"

"Okay, send her in."

Kena nodded, and Victor noticed her brief glance at Linc before she left the room. Victor shook his head, thinking, *Another one bites the dust.* He stood, buttoning his suit coat as Bella Deveraux entered the room.

"Detective?" he greeted.

"What's the plan, Governor?" Bella asked.

"The plan?"

"Don't do that, sir," Bella replied with narrowed eyes. "Taylor is my friend. For years, we put our lives in each other's hands. Whatever you got planned to get justice for her, I want in on it."

Victor didn't know Bella Deveraux from a can of paint. She said that she and Taylor were friends, and maybe they were, but Taylor had never mentioned her before. Nevertheless, something told him that she could be trusted. But, truth be told, he trusted Collier too, so he wasn't taking any chances. Yet, it seemed as though Lucas wasn't exercising nearly as much caution.

"He's heavily guarded. Our plan is to be patient," Lucas blurted.

Victor, along with his brothers, glared at Lucas as if he'd grown a second head, but he was so focused on the detective that he hadn't noticed. The look on Lucas' face reminded him of a character in the Saturday morning cartoons that he used to watch when he was younger. Victor pictured Lucas' eyes popping out of his head and his eyeballs rolling

CREED

by *Phoenix Daniels*

around like marbles. He would have laughed if Lucas wasn't being led by his other head.

"Detective Deveraux, will you excuse us?" Victor asked.

"No," she replied bluntly, shaking her head.

"No?" Victor repeated, surprised by her response.

"No, sir. I mean no disrespect, but I put three bullets in that asshole, and he's alive. I… I left him alive," she said, jamming her finger into her chest. "I want in on what's going down."

Victor had to admit that he was shocked by her hardcore passion. And as much as he was shocked, it seemed his brother was turned on. He could actually hear Lucas' breathing increase. The woman was talking about committing murder, but Lucas was smitten.

"Detective, will you at least, agree to revisit this when Taylor is out of the woods?" Victor asked, still staring at his brother.

She looked over at Lucas and gave him the subtlest of smiles, before turning to Victor.

"Yes, sir. That's understandable. Just, please, don't leave me out of the loop."

"I won't. I promise," Victor assured.

Bella peeked over at Lucas one last time before turning to leave the room. Even Victor noticed the sway of her hips in the skinny jeans that she was wearing. Hell, she was very fit, and he was, after all, a man. And it wasn't shit wrong with his vision. She didn't have the curves that his woman had, but her curves were peek worthy.

When she closed the door behind herself, Lucas threw his head back and groaned.

CREED

by *Phoenix Daniels*

"Damn, God was good to that woman," he mumbled under his breath.

"Can we stay focused?" Victor grumbled.

"Oh, I focused in all right. My view of that ass was very clear," Lucas chuckled.

"You know… there's something wrong with the lot of you," Victor huffed.

"Whoa," Alexander interjected. "Jaysen and I have been perfect gentlemen."

"That's because you're both damn near married," Lincoln scoffed.

"That's bullshit! I'm as single as you," Alexander countered.

"Who the fuck cares? We got bigger fish to fry," Victor reminded them.

Dealing with his horny brothers could be a handful, but he trusted no one else to do the things that he needed to be done. He trusted each of his brothers with his life. They would never betray him, and he would give his life for each of them, and they for him. Victor knew that when the hard things needed to get done, there were no better enforcers than the Creed brothers.

CHAPTER 28

TAYLOR

"Nooo!" Taylor screamed, waking with a terrifying startle. Her eyes darted frantically around the room. For a few seconds, she'd forgotten where she was. She grabbed the cold rails on the sides of the hospital bed and gasped, filling her burning lungs with air.

"It's okay, baby. I'm here. It's okay," Victor whispered. He gently wiped the sweat from her forehead and kissed the top of her head. "You're okay, Sweetness," he assured. "You're okay. It's just a dream."

"No, Victor. It wasn't just a dream," she breathlessly replied. "That bastard shot me."

"I know, but you're gonna be just fine."

Taylor closed her eyes allowed her head to fall back against the pillow. "Bella said that he made it through surgery. Where is he now?"

Victor hesitated, before saying, "Baby, please, don't worry about Collier. He's in custody."

"In this hospital?" she asked.

"Yes, but they're moving him to the Stroger today," Victor said, massaging her scalp.

"What time?"

As he continued to knead her scalp, Taylor could hear the change in his breathing.

"Taylor, baby, just please concentrate on getting better. Let me worry about Collier."

CREED
by *Phoenix Daniels*

Taylor nodded, hearing the failed attempt to disguise the irritation in his voice. She looked into the beautiful green eyes that had hypnotized her months ago, and he blessed her with a beautiful smile that not only reached his eyes but transformed his entire face. She marveled at his brilliant white teeth, dimples as deep as craters, and thick, lustrous lashes that most women would kill for.

"Okay, Governor, you win. I'll lie here and be a good little patient," she relented, smiling up at him.

"That's my girl. Now..." he said, pausing to kiss her forehead. "...You have a visitor."

"Who?"

"You'll see."

He backed away from her bed and opened the door to her room. Taylor's hand flew to her mouth and tears welled in her eyes as Maria wheeled herself into Taylor's room. Other than being in a wheelchair, she looked like her normal self.

"So instead of going out there and finding the motherfucka that shot me, you go and get yourself shot," Maria quipped.

"Oh my God, Maria, you look amazing."

Maria's smile was cocky. "Of course, I do."

Taylor was overwhelmed with emotion, elated to see her friend up and alert. She couldn't suppress the tears falling from her eyes.

Victor cleared his throat from the doorway. "I'm gonna let you two catch up. I'll be close by if you need me."

"Okay, baby. I'll see you later."

CHAPTER 29

CREED

Victor joined his brothers in the hospital's conference room.

"Okay, we don't have much time. They're moving that son of a bitch in an hour," he told them.

"I got it covered," Linc assured. "We'll intercept him on the way. You stay with your lady. We'll handle this."

"Linc, please, keep in mind that he's got information that we need," Jaysen implored, staring pointedly at Lincoln.

"I'm well aware of that, Jay. Why do you feel you need to tell me that?"

"So you don't kill him," Lucas blurted.

Lincoln crossed his arms over his chest and frowned at his brothers. But he remained silent.

"Seriously, Linc, don't kill him," Victor warned.

"What the fuck?! I look like Charles Fucking Manson to you assholes?" Lincoln huffed.

"Naw, man," Alexander interceded. "They're just asking you to check your temper just long enough for us to get the answers we need, then you can go Rambo."

"Rambo, huh?" Lincoln asked, feigning offense.

"Yes, Rambo," Victor confirmed, walking over to his younger brother.

"That's funny, Vic, but maybe you should inform your little brothers that you're way more dangerous than I've ever been? They seem to think that the good governor is a bit soft."

CREED
by *Phoenix Daniels*

"Bullshit," Alexander chuckled. "I'm a lot of things, but stupid ain't one of them."

Victor smirked at Alex and grabbed Lincoln by the back of his neck and planted a kiss on his forehead. His brother was definitely a rough-neck, but Victor loved him dearly. Lincoln was loyal to a fault; he'd die for the people he loved and the country he served.

Linc slapped him on the back and pushed him away. "We need to get going, Vic. Go back to your lady. Once we secure the package, we'll save it for you."

"Yeah, okay, thank you... all of you," Victor said, sincerely.

The brothers filed out of the conference room only to be met in the hall by an angry Bella Deveraux.

"Did you do it?" Her tone was accusatory. Victor, along with his brothers stared at her, with no idea of what she was referring to.

"Detective, what are you talking about?" Victor asked.

"Collier!" she shouted in a whisper. "His throat was slashed from ear to ear."

As she spoke, she was obviously studying their reactions.

"Fuck!" Victor shouted.

Suddenly, all of the brothers simultaneously looked over at Lincoln.

"What?! I didn't do it. That asshole had damn near the entire police department guarding his room. How the hell would I get to him?"

Victor shook his head. Although he knew that his brother had nothing to do with Collier's murder, he knew that

CREED
by *Phoenix Daniels*

Lincoln could've totally gotten to him if he wanted. He all but admitted that he could. But the truth was, Lincoln would've claimed his work. Nonetheless, Victor couldn't even begin to hide his disappointment. Getting answers would be harder than he anticipated.

"Detective, it wasn't us trust me," Victor assured.

"Shit!" Bella swore. "Now we'll never find out who the fuck this *she* is."

"We will," Victor promised with conviction.

He nodded at Gregor, who was waiting patiently across the hall. Together, they walked back to Taylor's room. As he opened the door, he thought about Taylor. He wondered if she were physically able, would his woman be capable of slicing a man's throat.

He concluded. *Without a doubt.*

Taylor

Taylor rested against the pillow as Maria went on and on about Michael's pathetic attempts to reconcile. Supposedly, he'd learned the error of his ways. But according to Maria, it was a done deal. When Maria was unconscious, Taylor witnessed Michael's remorsefulness first hand. Maybe he was just a damn good actor, but Taylor didn't think so. His pain seemed sincere.

Maria took a paper towel and wiped the sweat from her forehead. She stared in the mirror for a bit before returning to her wheelchair and rolling her way over to Taylor's bedside.

"Maria, correct me if I'm wrong... You're a devout Catholic, are you not?"

"Um-hm," she responded with narrowed eyes.

"And... being a devout Catholic, divorce is out of the question. Is it not?"

"Yeah, counselor. What's your point?"

"My point is... you're stuck with that motherfucka. So, you may as well make it work."

"Thank you, Dr. Phil," Maria grumbled. "How about you let-"

Just as Maria was about to read Taylor, Victor entered the room with his four drool-worthy brothers in tow. Taylor's own breath hitched by their presence. She instinctively ran her fingers through her wild hair; a reaction to being in a room with so many beautiful men. She smiled shyly when Victor's eyes went narrow.

CREED
by *Phoenix Daniels*

"Oh… my… fucking… God," Taylor could hear Maria mumble under her breath. Taylor smiled and waggled her brows at her friend. Victor chuckled softly and introduced Maria to his brothers. Taylor laughed on the inside as Maria tripped over her words, stuttering a greeting.

"Taylor, these are my brothers," Victor said with a wave toward the group of tall, handsome men. "They just wanted to come by and say hello. This is Lucas, Lincoln, Alexander, and the puny one is Jaysen."

"Puny?" Jaysen protested.

Taylor giggled. Surely, Victor was making a funny. There was nothing puny about Jaysen. He had to be at least 6'7".

"It's nice to meet you all," Taylor greeted with enthusiasm.

What started out as a "quick visit," had gone into well over an hour. Taylor loved the witty banter between the brothers. They were having such a good time that Taylor forgot that she was in a hospital. And since Alexander had positioned himself behind Maria's wheelchair, and they seemed to be sharing private jokes, Maria appeared to be enjoying the visit as well.

After a while, the nurse had come in and threatened to throw everyone out, but Victor had turned his steely gaze on the poor woman, causing her to cower and back out of the room. Taylor felt sorry for the woman. She looked over at Victor and mouthed, "Bully." Victor only shrugged and rejoined the boisterous conversation. They laughed loudly as Lincoln regaled them with childhood stories.

CREED
by *Phoenix Daniels*

The door flew open and in walked Tabitha Creed. The room became instantly silent. She folded her arms and frowned at the group.

Taylor cleared her throat, breaking the silence. "Dr. Creed, this is my friend and partner, Maria Mendez."

"Hello, Maria. How are you feeling?"

"I'm doing pretty good, Dr. Creed. It's nice to meet you."

Dr. Creed smiled, but her smile disappeared when she turned to her sons. "These women are here to recover. You need to go and find somewhere else to play."

Taylor noticed that the steely look that Victor gave the nurse hadn't made an appearance with Tabitha Creed. As a matter of fact, none of the brothers said a word.

"Out," Tabitha ordered, waving at the door.

The men filed out quietly. Taylor could see Victor's reluctance to leave. He hovered over her bed quietly, hoping that his mother hadn't meant to include him in the eviction. Taylor was amused. She had *never* seen anyone handle Victor.

Tabitha studied Victor a few seconds before turning to Maria. She walked over to the wheelchair, saying, "Darling, I'm going to take you back to your room. If you're going to get stronger, you'll need your rest."

"Yes ma'am," Maria said in a small voice. At that moment, Taylor could picture Maria as a little girl.

Tabitha gripped the handles and rolled Maria toward the door.

"I'll see you later, Maria," Taylor called out.

Maria waved, responding with, "Later."

CREED
by *Phoenix Daniels*

Once they were alone, Taylor looked up at Victor and laughed.

"What are you laughing at?"

"You," Taylor giggled. "You and your brothers. You're all *'me Tarzan, you Jane'* until your mommy walks in."

Taylor was laughing uncontrollably, despite the pain in her chest.

"Ha ha. Are you done yet?" Victor grumbled.

"No. You guys are all giants; mountains of testosterone and that little woman came in here a shut it down," Taylor chuckled.

"Trust me; she's a lot taller than she appears," Victor retorted with a grand smile.

"Yeah. I can see that. She's a force."

"That she is," he affirmed.

CREED

by *Phoenix Daniels*

CHAPTER 30

TAYLOR

Two months later…

Taylor raised her face toward the warmth of the sun. It was unseasonably warm for autumn. She and Victor were strolling through the exquisite gardens of the Executive Mansion. She'd been in Springfield since she was released from the hospital. Victor had insisted that she recover in the Governor's Mansion, claiming that the abundance of staff could provide Taylor with whatever help she needed. But Taylor knew that, for Victor, it was all about safety. The Executive Mansion had security everywhere.

"Are you looking forward to going back to the city tonight?" Victor asked.

"Yeah. But I'm not looking forward to court tomorrow," Taylor admitted.

Taylor was no longer in pain, and her strength and energy had returned. She was feeling more and more like her old self. It was time to go home.

Victor tugged her hand and pulled her against his side. Draping an arm over her shoulder, he held her tight and kissed the top of her head.

"I have a surprise for you," he muttered against her hair.

"Really? What is it?"

"A surprise," he reiterated. "Come with me."

CREED
by *Phoenix Daniels*

He led her to a pathway that led to the back of the
property. Taylor was apprehensive. She didn't like surprises,
but she kept that to herself.

Behind the estate was a garage the size of a small home.
Victor opened the door and led her inside. It was so dark that
Taylor couldn't see her hand in front of her face. She stayed as
close to Victor as possible, until he flipped the switch,
activating the lights. His beautiful smile came into focus.
Victor's extreme good looks often made Taylor's heart race.

"Victor, you're so beautiful," she gushed, caressing his
jaw.

"You think so?" he asked with a mischievous glint in his
eyes.

"I'll bet that I'm not as beautiful as this," he said,
grabbing her shoulders and turning her toward her surprise.
Taylor gasped. Her hand flew to her mouth, and her heart
skipped a beat. Just before her was a brand-new Ducati Monster
1200R. It was jet black and chromed from throttle to clutch. She
took tentative steps toward the beautiful motorcycle and placed
a gentle hand on the seat.

"Oh… my… God! Victor, this is amazing!"

"You know that I both love and hate seeing you on a
motorcycle, but I know how much you love to ride. Just
promise me you'll be careful."

Taylor turned and flew into Victor's arms, giving him a
gigantic bear hug.

"I promise. I'll be careful. I promise. Thank you so
much, baby. I love it. I love you," she rambled.

Victor laughed and leaned into her.

CREED
by *Phoenix Daniels*

"I love you too, sweetness," he said before covering her lips with his own.

The kiss started out sweet and tender, but it developed into something more urgent; more passionate. Taylor purred against his lips and gripped his muscular back. She found herself rubbing against him like a cat in heat. Since she was recovering from a gunshot wound, it had been months since they'd made love, and Taylor was in the worst kind of need. Without ending the kiss, Victor slowly walked her backward to the hood of a limousine.

"Can you do this?" he asked against her lips.

"Yes," she breathed. "I need you, Victor."

"You're sure?"

"Yes. I'm sure."

Victor took his time ridding her of her clothing. Taylor stood naked before him, feeling not in the least bit vulnerable. Even as Victor stood, fully dressed, Taylor understood that she was safe with him. She could see the appreciation in his expression as he perused her nude form. He ran a gentle finger over the scar left by a madman's bullet.

"I'll never let anything happen to you again," he promised. "I would, with no hesitation, die for you, Taylor."

"Nobody's dying, Victor. Now, baby, please…I need you," Taylor implored.

Victor smiled and started peeling away his own clothing. Taylor couldn't look away as he revealed muscle after solid muscle. As he stood naked in front of her, Taylor marveled at his extreme masculinity. His beauty equivalent to the Statue of David, but with a bigger dick.

CREED
by *Phoenix Daniels*

Victor closed in on Taylor, pushing his fingers through her hair and pressing his lips to hers. Taylor's arms snaked around his neck, but he quickly removed them, placing them behind her, palms down on the hood of the limo.

"Keep them there," he ordered, planting sensual kisses to her face, neck, and then the scar on her chest. Taylor's head dropped backward. Her breathing became shallow as Victor made his way to her erected nipple. He licked a slow circle around the tight pebble, before drawing it into his mouth. Taylor drew in a sharp breath. She could feel moisture instantly pooling in her core. Victor continued to lick and flick at her hardened nipples, sending torturous and intense jolts of pleasure to the bundle of nerves. Taylor's moans echoed throughout the garage. She squirmed against the limo as she struggled to keep her palms on the hood. Victor rotated between nipples, providing the same torturous teasing to each. He prompted her legs apart and rubbed tantalizing circles into her hot, swollen sex.

"Victor," she breathed.

"Victor, what?" he dared. "Do you want me to fuck you? Or do you want me to eat this sweet pussy?"

"Fuck me, baby. Please fuck me," she pleaded.

"Yeah, okay, sweetness."

But Victor wasn't in the spirit of compliance. He dropped to his knees and captured Taylor's throbbing, swollen clit between his lips. He moaned pleasurably at the first taste of her in months and began to feverishly lick her begging pussy.

"Fuuuuck!" Taylor shouted without shame. "Ooooh.... fuck!"

CREED
by *Phoenix Daniels*

Victor worked her over with his mouth until her legs began to tremble. Just as they were about to give out, he pushed her back against the hood of the limo and spread her trembling legs apart. He stroked his swollen dick, preparing to enter. And even though Taylor was just as caught up in the moment as he, she held out her hand and halted his entry.

"We don't have protection," she warned.

"I know," he grunted as he entered her warm center.

Taylor groaned from the sheer pleasure of his wet, raw dick inside of her.

"Victor, I could get pregnant."

"I'm counting on it," he grumbled, pushing deep inside.

"Victor!" Taylor gasped. "Oh shit, Victor!"

"You're mine, sweetness. I'm putting my baby in here," Victor informed as he pounded her insides. "My son," he grunted as he fucked her with aggression.

Beads of sweat accumulated on his forehead.

"Yesss!" Taylor screamed as he fucked her recklessly. "Ugh! Yes!"

Taylor rose to the absolute highest of heights, but then she fell… hard. An explosive orgasm ripped through her and tore her to shreds. She collapsed against the automobile, clutching Victor's shoulders, and gasping for air. Victor was riding her roughly, reaching his peak. He propelled into her one last time, before expelling his seed.

"Oh… my… G…" she choked as his hot cum pulsed inside of her. Victor struggled to catch his breath and collapsed on top of her. He rose to his elbows and looked her deeply in the eye.

"I love you," he panted against her temple.

CREED
by *Phoenix Daniels*

CHAPTER 31

CREED

Fifteen minutes into the ride from Victor's penthouse, Taylor hadn't spoken a word. Victor could tell by her demeanor that she didn't want him to accompany her to court, but Taylor's attitude was of no concern to Victor. He had made a promise with his life that he wouldn't allow anything else to happen to her. It was a promise that he intended to make good on. If he lost Taylor, he would lose everything that was good in his life.

They were on their way to the Cook County courthouse for Gore's preliminary hearing. A judge would determine if there was enough evidence to charge the officer with murder. Taylor and Maria were the prosecution's star witnesses.

Victor knew all too well that she was not looking forward to testifying against her peer. But admirably, Taylor decided to tell the truth, regardless of the damage that being honest would do to her relationships with other cops. She was putting her own moral code before the silent code that most officers shared. Most cops would've just backed up their fellow officer, but Taylor and Maria were remarkably strong and honorable women. And whatever happened, Victor intended to have their backs. Still, he could tell that Taylor didn't want him there. And if she didn't want *him* present, she was going to be downright pissed by his brothers' presence.

CREED

by *Phoenix Daniels*

Taylor instructed the driver to pull across the street from the courthouse to an employee parking lot.

"No, sweetness. You forget, I'm the governor. We park in front."

"Fine," Taylor huffed in an exasperated tone.

Victor closed in on her and enclosed her face in his hands. He looked into her beautiful brown eyes and assured her that everything would work out okay.

Taylor gave him a weak smile, before dropping her head. "I'm okay, babe, really. I've testified in court thousands of times. I got this. Trust me."

"I do trust you, Taylor. But just in case, I'll be sitting right in the back of the courtroom."

"Victor, I don't need a babysitter," Taylor grumbled as she climbed out of the SUV.

Victor climbed out after her. "Yes, you do. Let's go," he mused, giving her ass a little swat.

He grabbed her hand and raised it to his lips. "Stop fuss'n," he said, imitating her father, forcing a giggle from Taylor.

As they climbed the court steps, reporters began to swarm, but Victor's security detail blocked their paths. When they entered the courthouse, Taylor flashed her badge and detoured around the metal detector. Victor waited as his security team flashed badges of their own. Once through security, they headed to the correct courtroom.

"Victor, I can take it from here," Taylor told him, pulling her hand from his.

Victor looked down at their severed connection and then to Taylor. After all the time they'd spent together, Victor couldn't believe that Taylor was still uncomfortable being his woman.

"Okay, sweetheart. You go on in. I'll hang back."

Taylor raised to her toes to kiss him, and Victor could see instant relief wash over her. As she entered the courtroom without him, he wasn't hurt or offended. Victor realized that Taylor valued her independence and wanted all, if any, advancements to be achieved by her own merit. But, sadly, Taylor hadn't realized that that ship had sailed. She would always be linked to him, and for that, Victor felt a tad bit guilty.

CREED

by *Phoenix Daniels*

TAYLOR

Taylor entered the courtroom and walked down what felt like a mile-long aisle; one side filled with cops, and the other, angry citizens. Neither side seemed to have much love for Taylor. She looked back, regretting her decision to not allow Victor to walk in with her. He stood tall and confident in the back of the courtroom, flanked by his brothers. His encouraging smile boosted her own confidence. Taylor smiled in return and continued down the aisle. She took a seat next to Maria, ignoring loud whispers about her relationship with Victor, her shooting an unarmed man, and her being a rat.

"Ugh," Taylor groaned.

"Yep," Maria said with a nod. "This is where we are."

Before Taylor could respond, Candace Wallace took the seat next to Taylor.

"Damn. Isn't this some shit?" Candace mumbled.

Taylor hadn't seen Candace since she warned them that Gore was stripped of all of his police powers, charged with murder, and out for blood.

"I know, right?" Taylor huffed.

"Tell me something, Tay. If you could go back in time, would you change your statement?"

"Nope," Taylor responded, without hesitation.

"Well, I'm here to support you guys. And I ain't the only one in your corner. Y'all did the right thing."

"Thanks, Candace," Taylor responded sincerely.

Taylor looked across the courtroom to find Jim Gore and his partner, Trevor Hall, staring daggers at her. If looks could kill,

CREED
by *Phoenix Daniels*

they would have surely finished the job that she suspected they started with shooting her *and* Maria. Taylor didn't look away; she couldn't. She refused to show weakness. So the stare down continued until the Cook County Sheriff demanded, "ALL RISE."

CREED
by *Phoenix Daniels*

CHAPTER 32

TAYLOR

As far as preliminary hearings went, Gore's went by fairly quickly. The prosecutor had decided to use Taylor and Maria's signed statements, saving their actual testimonies for trial. And ultimately, the judge found that there was sufficient probable cause and set a date for trial.

Taylor and Maria walked out of the courtroom, into the hall where Victor and his brothers were waiting. Standing with them were Kena and a pretty Black woman that Taylor had never seen before.

"Mm... mm... mm," Candace said as she approached.

"Girl, I know," Maria replied under her breath.

"It's like Magic Mike XXL in this motherfucker," Candace chuckled. "How do you stay on your feet? I'm fucking swooning over here."

Taylor laughed out loud and told her, "It's easy for me, 'cause I only have eyes for one man."

"Hmph! Well, I see every last one of 'em," Maria quipped.

"Introduce me," Candace whispered.

"Uhm... okay."

Taylor walked over to the group with a smile on her face. The Creed brothers were a supportive bunch. She wasn't at all surprised when she saw them in the courtroom. Since she'd been shot, one or the other was charged with keeping her

CREED
by *Phoenix Daniels*

safe when Victor was away on business. Taylor also suspected that they were secretly keeping an eye on Maria as well.

"Hey, guys," Taylor said as she walked up to the group.

She hugged each of them and thanked them for coming. After gracing her with the typical Creed banter, Taylor introduced Candace to the group. After a round of polite greetings and a lot of flirting on Candace's part, Victor placed his hand in the small of Taylor's back and directed her attention to the unknown woman.

"Taylor, I'd like you to meet Renee Griffin."

"Renee!" Taylor greeted with excitement. "I've heard such great things about you. Thanks for keeping the citizens from charging my gates."

"Likewise. It's good to finally meet you, Taylor. I'm happy to help," Renee responded with the same excitement.

"Renee is holding a press conference tonight regarding the hearing," Victor interjected.

"Really? Why?" Taylor asked, surprised.

"Well, the plan is to get ahead of the press and the police department on this. Go on the offensive, instead of fending off another attack," Renee explained.

"A preemptive strike before that asshole, Brent Trainer, muddies the waters," Victor added.

"Sounds like a good plan to me," Maria chimed.

"Fine, as long as I don't have to speak," Taylor agreed. "I'm sure you know what you're doing."

"That I do," Renee responded with a smile.

"That being said…" Candace interjected. "… Why don't the three of us do some catching up? Dinner at my place?"

CREED

by *Phoenix Daniels*

Taylor glanced at Victor, assessing his reaction to Candace's invitation. It wasn't that she needed his permission. She just wasn't in a debating mood. Plus, she didn't want him to worry. She could already see the battle raging behind his eyes. But, to Taylor's surprise, he smiled. "Security should be able to handle you having dinner with your friends. Besides, I'd hate to be the idiot that barged in on three armed and dangerous women."

Laughter was emanating from the small group when Taylor pulled Victor away. "What will you do tonight?" she asked him.

"I'm going to the office. I have some work to catch up on. Listen, babe. Don't worry about me. Go and have fun with your girlfriends," he encouraged.

"And... you're sure?"

"I'm sure, sweetness," Victor assured. "I know that I've been crazy overprotective. It's only because I love you. But I don't want to make you feel like a prisoner. Just promise me that you won't do anything to put yourself at risk."

"I promise. And I don't feel like a prisoner. I feel loved."

"Good," he said, pulling her against him.

He gently tugged her hair, pulling her head back, and giving himself better access to her lips. He kissed her gently and muttered, "Go. Have fun."

"Yes, governor. Thank you, sir."

Victor's sexy grin revealed dimples that were too cute for a man as hard as him. Despite the hell that Taylor had been through in the past months, with Victor, she was truly happy. In fact, she was happier than she'd ever been. Yes, he was

CREED
by *Phoenix Daniels*

stubborn and overprotective. But more than that, he was kind, loving, and unselfish in every way. As he ushered her back to her friends, Taylor silently thanked God for putting him in her life.

"Are we hanging?" Candace asked eagerly, upon Taylor's return.

"We're hanging," Taylor confirmed. "Maria?"

"I'm in," Maria concurred.

As the ladies headed toward the exit, accompanied by a small security detail, Taylor shouted over her shoulder, "Gregor, take care of my man!"

"Will do, miss lady," he shouted in return.

Taylor walked out of the courthouse with her friends, smiling as she thought of the amount of alcohol that they were going to consume that evening.

CREED
by *Phoenix Daniels*

VICTOR

Victor dropped the budget sheet on his desk and glanced at the phone. He was resisting the urge to call Taylor. He'd all but ordered her to go out and have fun, but he couldn't help the uneasy feeling that he had when she wasn't with him. He'd made several calls to Henry Finn, the head of Taylor's security detail. Henry had assured him that the ladies were inside, and all was quiet, so Victor did his best not to worry.

He rose from his chair and walked over to the large window that overlooked downtown Chicago. The view from his office was mesmerizing.

So beautiful, yet so violent, he marveled.

He imagined Taylor running through the city streets, chasing bad guys, and thought of a number of more suitable careers. He would definitely pull some strings. But Victor was no fool. He knew all too well that Taylor wasn't the sort to be handled. If he so much as mentioned her leaving her job, she'd bite his head off. Unfortunately for her, Victor didn't play fair. If push came to shove, he'd just have her fired.

Just as he was beginning to feel guilt for his controlling nature, Kena entered his office.

"Governor, Detective Deveraux is here to see you. She says it's urgent."

"Send her in," Victor grumbled.

He turned away from the window and shoved his hands into his pockets, preparing himself for another interrogation from Bella Deveraux. Over the past couple of months, she'd been relentlessly investigating Collier's murder. She'd not only

CREED

by *Phoenix Daniels*

questioned him, but Taylor, Maria, and all of his brothers as well; several times. In Victor's opinion, she was just angry because she hadn't gotten to Collier first.

Bella entered his office, and something about her behavior gave Victor pause. She seemed almost panicked.

"Detective?"

"Governor, have you spoken to Taylor this evening?" she blurted.

Definitely panicked.

"What's happened?" Victor asked urgently.

"I've been trying to contact Taylor. Her phone is going straight to voicemail."

Victor closed the distance between them, looked her straight in the eye and asked a bit more forcefully, "What's going on, Detective Deveraux?"

"I have information… And I've been trying to contact Taylor and Maria, but I can't get an answer from either of them. Both phones are going straight to voicemail."

"They're together, and Taylor has a security detail. I've spoken with the head of her detail. He says that the ladies are fine."

Bella visibly relaxed.

"Do you know who *she* is?" Victor asked.

"Well…," she hesitated. "I really need to talk to them. Do you know where they are?" she asked, blatantly ignoring his question.

"Who is *she*?" Victor asked again.

"I'm sorry, governor. I can't give you information on an on-going investigation," she actually had the nerve to say.

"Detective Deveraux, who the fuck is *she*?"

CREED
by *Phoenix Daniels*

Bella stood to her full height, squared her shoulders, and said to him, "Governor, you don't intimidate me."

"Detective Deveraux, if you keep screwing around with me, the only thing that you'll be investigating from this day forward is how to file for unemployment. Don't fuck with me; not when it comes to Taylor."

Bella's eyes narrowed, but Victor could tell that she was relenting. But he was certain that it was more out of concern for Taylor and Maria than a fear of him. He was sure that Belladonna Deveraux wasn't easily intimidated.

"Look, Governor, I'll tell you everything that I know. Just, please, tell me where they are."

"They're having dinner at a friend's house; another cop. Her name is Candace."

Bella's mouth flew open at the mention of Candace's name. Her eyes widened, and her golden complexion actually grew flushed.

"Oh, God," she gasped.

Now it was Victor who was bordering panic.

"*She* is Candace?" Victor asked, terrified of the answer.

Bella turned and bolted to the door, shouting, "Call your security detail and tell them to get Taylor and Maria outta there!"

CREED

by *Phoenix Daniels*

CHAPTER 33

TAYLOR

"Dinner was great," Taylor complimented.

"Yeah," Candace scoffed. "That's 'cause I didn't cook it. My mom brought the food over earlier today."

"Thank God for mothers," Maria chortled.

"Yeah. Tell me about it. More wine?" Candace offered, tossing her thick blond hair over her shoulder.

"Duh," Taylor answered chuckle.

Candace poured the last of the wine into Taylor's glass.

"I'll go grab another bottle," she said as she walked into the kitchen.

"You enjoying yourself?" Taylor asked Maria.

Candace was Taylor's friend from the academy. Maria only knew her through Taylor, but they seemed to get along well.

"Yeah. It's good to be out of the house. Since the shooting, neither my husband nor your man will give me a minute to myself. Between my man's hovering, and your man's—"

"I *knew* he put a detail on you! *I knew it!*"

"Ya think he didn't?" Maria scoffed, rolling her eyes.

"He means well," Taylor defended.

"I know. He's sweet. Well… not sweet, per se. I wouldn't exactly call Victor Creed sweet, but he is… um… well, you know."

CREED
by *Phoenix Daniels*

"I know," Taylor responded with a nod.

"So…" Candace called from the kitchen. "Do either of you feel the least bit guilty about not backing Gore's story?"

"Not in the least," Maria responded, taking a sip of wine.

Taylor, perplexed by the question, asked, "Why would we?"

Candace entered the dining room with another bottle of wine. Taylor was wondering why Candace would repeatedly question their decision to tell the truth about the shooting, especially when she claimed to have had their backs. When Candace placed the bottle on the table, something in her expression rubbed Taylor the wrong way. Was she masking anger?

"Well, because, we're supposed to look out for each other. You know… back each other's play."

"What?" Maria asked with a frown, sitting her glass on the table.

"Why the fuck would we back that play? *We* didn't arrest him, charge him, or prosecute him. All we did was tell the truth. What the fuck is this?" Maria snapped.

Taylor sat back and quietly listened to the exchange. Candace's mask had slipped, and Taylor watched as she tried to put it back on.

"Damn, chica, calm down. I was just saying out loud what a lot of cops are thinking. Don't shoot the messenger," Candace chuckled, holding her hands up in surrender.

"And you think we need you to tell us what people are thinking? You wanna know what I suspect? I suspect that you're one of *those* people."

CREED

by *Phoenix Daniels*

"Listen, Maria, I was just asking a question. I'm sorry if I offended you."

"Well, you-," Maria's rebuttal was cut off by a loud ring.

"That's me," Candace said, jumping up from the table.

She ran to the counter and picked up her phone. Taylor looked over at Maria, who had turned beet red, and her expression was murderous.

"I say we call it a night," Taylor suggested.

"Good idea," Maria huffed.

They stood from the table and went to gather their things.

"Don't go," Candace said as she brushed past them. "That was my old man. He can't get past your security. I'm gonna go get him."

Even that statement was dripping with hostility as far as Taylor was concerned. As Candace hurried out of the front door, Taylor noted that her behavior was bordering manic.

"Our purses are missing," Maria revealed, pointing at the sofa. "We put our purses right here."

The hairs on the back of Taylor's neck stood at attention as she heard the creak of the front door opening and closing. Candace entered the living room, brandishing a smirk that was diabolical.

"Going somewhere?" she asked in a tone coated with hatred.

Entering the living room behind her was none other than, Jim Gore.

"What the fuck is this?" he hissed, as soon as he saw Taylor and Maria.

CREED
by *Phoenix Daniels*

"Yeah, what the fuck is this?!" Maria shouted.

"Shut the fuck up! You border jumping wetback!" Candace screamed.

"Who the fuck are you callin' a wetback?! You White-trash, leaky, cunt!" Maria shouted in return.

Candace pulled a gun from the back of her pants and pointed it at Maria. "You bitch! I'm talking to you. You should have died when I dropped two bullets in your back."

Rage emanated from Maria. Her breathing became harsh, and she was seconds away from charging at Candace. Taylor grabbed her wrist and gave it a squeeze, a reminder to Maria that Candace was pointing a loaded weapon at them.

"Whoa, Candy, what the fuck are you doing?" Gore asked, moving between them.

"I'm saving your ass!" she screeched.

"Saving my ass?"

"Yeah. I'm eliminating the threat," she explained, as if he had asked a dumb question.

Her eyes darted frantically from Gore to Maria. And since Taylor wasn't Candace's main focus, she secretly searched the room for anything that could be used as a weapon.

"So, let me get this straight… you're saving my ass by kidnapping the only two people in the world whose demise would automatically be blamed on me?"

Candace didn't respond to his sarcastically posed question. Instead, she narrowed her eyes at Gore and spat, "You ungrateful son of a bitch! After all the years that we've been together, you still don't appreciate shit that I do for you."

"Do something that ain't gonna get me the gotdamn electric chair!" he roared. "Yeah, I fucked up at work, but that

CREED
by *Phoenix Daniels*

shit was an accident; nerves and shit. I could've fought that. I was on-duty. At worst, I could've been convicted of manslaughter; done five years. But this shit… ain't no coming back from this. You're on your own. I suggest you let them bitches go," Gore rattled off, turning toward the door. However, he was unable to make it out of the door before Candace turned her weapon to him and fired a round into his back.

"You. Ungrateful. Piece. Of. Shit," she gritted, as she fired another round into Jim Gore's back. Without so much as a whisper to each other, Taylor and Maria were definitely speaking the same language as they simultaneously rushed Candace. But she quickly turned and fired in their direction. They both froze. Taylor instinctively clutched her chest, searching for injuries. She looked over to check Maria, but she appeared to be unharmed. When Taylor turned back to Candace, she was in the sitting position on the floor, with her back leaning against the wall. To Taylor's surprise, she had what appeared to be an entry wound, made by a bullet, in the center of her forehead. Brain matter was splattered all over the wall behind her. Taylor looked to Maria a second time, but she was just as confused and shocked as Taylor.

"Did she... shoot herself?" Maria asked.

"I-I don't-." Taylor stuttered.

"No," a voice called from behind.

Taylor, startled, turned to find not only Bella, but Victor *and* Linc.

"It was the gun-toting governor," Bella remarked, jerking a thumb at Victor.

Lincoln chuckled. Seemingly, not in the least bit affected by the bloodshed.

CREED
by *Phoenix Daniels*

"Victor," Taylor gasped, not running, but more like stumbling in his direction.

Thankfully, he was already making his way over to her.

"Are you hurt, baby?"

"N-no. I'm okay. Wow... what the fuck?"

"Governor, is that weapon registered to you?" Bella asked.

"Yes, ma'am," Victor confirmed.

Bella closed her eyes in frustration and ran her fingers through her straight black hair.

"Detective, this isn't gonna be a problem," Lincoln assured.

"Is that right?" she challenged.

"Yeah. I mean... he did save their lives."

Bella threw her head back, looked at the ceiling, and grumbled, "This is gonna be a paperwork nightmare."

CREED
by *Phoenix Daniels*

CHAPTER 33

VICTOR

Five hours later, surrounded by security, Victor, Taylor, Kena and his attorneys were finally leaving the Area South Detective's Division. Victor had been questioned for hours. And Bella was right; she had ended up completing a mountain of paperwork. As a witness to the incident, Bella corroborated his account of what went down.

"Governor, the press is out there," Gregor warned.

"Yeah, I figured that they would be," Victor grumbled.

He looked over at the front desk at several uniformed officers that were openly staring; apparently, thoroughly entertained by the media circus.

"Get the Chicago superintendent on the phone," he instructed Kena.

Kena retrieved her phone from her purse and made the call. Once the connection was made, she handed the phone to Victor.

"O'Conner, I'm quite sure that you're aware that I'm at the south side detective's division."

"Yes, sir, I am aware," Paul O'Conner responded.

"And you didn't think that the governor of Illinois shooting and killing a woman…a cop no less, would attract the media?"

"Y-yes, sir. I'm sorry, sir. I-."

"Get someone out here to control the press!" Victor shouted into the phone.

CREED
by *Phoenix Daniels*

"Yes, sir. I-."

Victor stabbed the end button, uninterested in listening to the superintendent grovel. Victor had already considered it disrespectful that O'Conner hadn't come to the station when he found out he was being questioned.

Seconds later, officers hurried from behind the desk and out the front doors. Other officers ran from closed offices to assist the desk officers in holding off reporters.

"You're mean," Taylor mumbled.

"And don't you forget it, sweetness. Let's go."

The officers created a distance of at least twenty feet between them and the press. They exited the building and walked the short distance to an awaiting SUV. Victor entered after Taylor and Kena. Gregor and Nate, his new driver, hopped in the front seat.

"Now that's power," Taylor mused.

"Yeah, baby, but with great power comes great responsibility," Victor pointed out.

"Kena, get in touch with Renee Griffin. Tell her to meet us at the penthouse."

"Already taken care of. She's waiting there for you now. I texted your parents and your brothers to let them know that you were okay, I approved the mayor's proposal on education reform for CPS, and I signed off on budget cuts for the Illinois Department of Transportation."

"Hmph. She's the one with all the power," Victor mused.

"And don't you forget it, sweetness," Kena mocked.

CREED

by *Phoenix Daniels*

* * * *

Finally, they were home. Victor had never felt such relief as he did when he watched Taylor make her way across the foyer and into the living room to plop down on the sofa. She threw her head back and sighed. He could've lost her, and that would've been unbearable. He walked over to the sofa and crouched down to a squat.

"Hey," he whispered to her.

"Hi," she responded, sluggishly.

"Do you want me to run you a bath?"

She looked over his shoulders at the small group waiting in the foyer.

"Naw, baby, I'll do it. Go take care of your business and then come to bed."

"Yes, ma'am. Don't wait up for me. Go to sleep," he ordered sweetly.

"Yes, governor. Goodnight."

"Goodnight, sweetheart."

They both stood. Victor watched as Taylor made her way to the bedroom. Once she disappeared from view, he turned to his staff. He did have business to take care of; starting with security.

"Finn!" he shouted. "How did Gore get into that house?"

Finn had the look of a deer caught in a set of headlights. He turned to the others for help, but they offered none. "Sir, he had a badge. H-he was a cop," Finn stammered.

CREED
by *Phoenix Daniels*

"Yeah, the very cop that Taylor was supposed to testify against! You're not doing security at Family Dollar! You're supposed to be the elite!"

"Governor, he had a badge. How was I supposed to know that he was the cop that was on trial?"

"Kena passed out a complete dossier on that asshole and his partner. Or maybe you could read a fucking paper! You... incompetent motherfucker!" Victor roared. "You're fired! Get the fuck out!"

Finn's eyes shone with defiance, but he was smart enough to turn and leave without a word. Once he was gone, Victor turned to Renee Griffin, his press secretary. "You got a plan?" he asked.

"Of course, I do, Governor," she replied with a smirk.

"Very good. Let's go into my office. Kenyatta, take the day off. Go home and sleep. Gregor switch shifts, lock up, and get some rest."

"Yes, sir," they said in unison.

CREED

by *Phoenix Daniels*

TAYLOR

Taylor rolled over and sank into the plushness of Victor's mattress, not at all in a hurry to get up. But she was starving, and the smell of food was luring her out of bed. She pushed back the comforter and scooted up the headboard.

Victor's deep sultry voice floated through the silence. "Good afternoon, sweetness," he greeted, causing an involuntary moan to escape from Taylor.

Victor was standing at the foot of the bed, fully dressed in one of his signature designer suits. His thick, dark hair was combed away from his handsome face, and his green eyes seemed to be glowing. Victor was tall, sexy, powerful, and holding a tray of food. He couldn't be more perfect. Taylor's stomach growled involuntarily as the delicious aroma tempted her senses. She rubbed her eyes and pushed her wild hair out of her face.

"Hey, baby. What time is it?" she asked. She could hear the hoarseness in her own voice.

Victor smiled and sat the tray on her lap. "It's almost two o'clock."

Taylor's eyes widened with surprise. "In the afternoon?"

"Yeah, but you were exhausted. You needed the sleep."

Taylor nodded and looked down at the tray of eggs, toast, bacon, and fruit. "Thanks, baby," she said, popping a grape into her mouth.

She bit into the grape and moaned out loud from the sweet explosion inside of her mouth.

CREED
by *Phoenix Daniels*

"Sweetness, you're making my dick hard," Victor warned.

"Yeah?"

"Mm-hm," he confirmed, massaging the swelling bulge that caused his slacks to stretch.

"Well, you don't look like you're ready for bed," Taylor teased seductively.

She wasn't opposed to rolling around in bed with him for an hour or two. But Victor wasn't cooperating. He removed his hand from his hard-on and stuffed his hands in the pockets.

"Eat," he demanded, walking around to sit on the other side of the bed.

Taylor rolled her eyes and grumbled, "Tease."

Victor had successfully gotten Taylor hot and bothered. Nevertheless, she began to attack the meal that he placed in front of her.

"I love watching you eat," Victor joked.

"Mm-hm," Taylor mumbled with a mouth full of food.

Taylor noticed that Victor had placed the newspaper on the tray. She debated in her mind about whether or not she should read it. Ultimately, she unfolded it and looked at the front page. The headline read:

GOVERNOR SAVES FIANCÈE'S LIFE!

"Fiancée'," Taylor scoffed. "At first, I was your married, cheating, girlfriend, and now I'm your fiancée?"

"That's what I'm hoping for," Victor proclaimed.

"What?" she asked, turning to face him.

Taylor's breath hitched at the sight of the black velvet box that Victor was holding. A shaky hand flew to her mouth as her heart raced uncontrollably.

CREED
by *Phoenix Daniels*

"Oh my God, Victor," Taylor breathed.

"Marry me, Taylor," he practically demanded, prompting Taylor to smile inside. "Make me the happiest man on earth."

A single tear trickled down her cheek. Victor had all but ordered her to marry him. It was just like her bossy man to do so. And even though they hadn't known each other that long, not marrying Victor wasn't an option. Taylor had no intention of spending the rest of her life without him.

"Yes, Victor, I'll marry you. I love you so fucking much," she declared.

"Well, then, I guess you can have this," Victor said with a chuckle.

He opened the small box, exposing a breathtaking princess cut solitaire, on a simple platinum band. The beauty and simplicity of the ring were…so Taylor. Beams of light reflecting from the gem danced around in Victor's beautiful eyes.

"Baby, it's gorgeous," Taylor gushed.

Victor took the ring out of the box and slipped it on her finger. She wasn't at all surprised that it fit perfectly; Victor didn't normally leave stones unturned. Taylor held her hand out in front of her, admiring her ring. She turned to Victor with narrowed her eyes, and asked, "Did you pick this ring out?"

"Girl, hell no," he admitted with a chuckle.

Taylor shook her head and laughed. "Then I guess I owe Kena dinner."

"Not this time," Victor countered. "This time, you owe my mom dinner."

CREED

by *Phoenix Daniels*

CHAPTER 34

TAYLOR

Taylor sat at the table in Louie's Chophouse, her mom's favorite restaurant, and nervously waited for her family to arrive. Even though they'd probably read it in the newspaper already, she and Victor had invited them to dinner to share the news of their engagement. Taylor was fidgeting with her engagement ring, twisting it around her finger, wondering how her parents would feel about her marrying Victor.

"Relax, sweetheart," Victor said, pulling her hands apart and placing one inside of his own. The warmth of his touch began to soothe her anxiety.

"I'm cool," Taylor lied.

"You're cool?" Victor asked suspiciously.

"Yep."

"Then why are you sitting over there looking like a teenager that's about to tell her parents that she's pregnant?" Victor asked with a chuckle.

Taylor sucked her teeth and playfully slapped his shoulder. "Hush. The only reason why your parents were so happy is because you're getting old and they don't have any grandkids."

Victor inhaled a sharp breath. "Old?!" he protested, feigning offense. "I got your old. I'm gonna show you old when I bend you over in my car tonight and fuck you until-."

Victor's dirty threat was interrupted when Nicole loudly cleared her throat, alerting them to her and her fiancé,

CREED
by *Phoenix Daniels*

Jeffrey's, presence. Taylor narrowed her eyes at Victor as she stood to hug her sister. The sexy smirk on his face told Taylor that he wasn't in the least embarrassed by what Jeffrey and Nicole may have heard.

"Nic, hey. Thanks for coming," she said as they embraced.

Victor stood and shook hands with Jeffrey and kissed Nicole on the cheek. Taylor greeted Jeffrey with a simple hello. Although he had never done anything to Taylor, she kept him at arm's length. She would never be rude or disrespectful to her sister's fiancé, but something about Jeffrey made Taylor feel uneasy. Maybe it wasn't even Jeffrey. Maybe it was the fact that he, without resistance, did whatever Nicole told him to do. To Taylor, it either diminished his manhood or revealed an ulterior motive. But it wasn't her place to speculate.

Before they could sit, Taylor spotted her parents entering the restaurant. She watched anxiously as the hostess escorted them to their table. Victor placed his hand in the small of Taylor's back. She took a deep breath, exhaled, and wondered why she was so nervous. Her family had always been supportive of her and her decisions. And as they approached with smiles, Taylor instantly relaxed.

"Hey, mommy, daddy," Taylor greeted with her arms outstretched, ready for warm hugs from the two people that loved her the most. And that's exactly what she got from both of her loving parents. After a warm, affectionate greeting with Victor, Nicole, and Jeffery, her parents took a seat.

"I love having us all together," Martha, Taylor's mom, pointed out as she placed a napkin on her lap.

"Me too, momma," Taylor agreed.

CREED
by *Phoenix Daniels*

"Mr. and Mrs. Montgomery-." Victor started before he was interrupted.

"Martha and James," Martha insisted. "Or… If the newspaper is correct, mom and dad."

Taylor turned to Victor and smiled, before sticking her hand out, showing off her engagement right.

"We're engaged!" Taylor announced with excitement.

"Congratulations!" everyone except Nicole shouted.

"Thank you. This daughter of yours made me a very happy man when she agreed to be my wife," Victor said as he placed Taylor's hand in his.

"Well, isn't that sweet," Nicole remarked without hiding her sarcasm.

Taylor didn't understand her sister's stank ass attitude. When Nicole announced her engagement to her yuppie fiancé, Taylor was nothing but supportive.

"What's your problem?" Taylor asked.

"Y'all just met a few months ago."

"Yep, and that ain't bothering us, so why is it an issue for you?"

"Whatever," Nicole dismissed. "If you like it I love it," Nicole mumbled.

"Well, I like it. So, chill the hell out. I didn't trip when you got engaged to *him*."

Nicole, clearly offended, gasped as she repeated Taylor's not so subtle slight against Jeffrey. "*Him*?"

"Okay, girls. That's enough!" Martha warned. "Cut it out!"

CREED
by *Phoenix Daniels*

Taylor stood abruptly. The sound of her chair scraping against the floor caused a few patrons to look curiously at their table. Victor stood as well. He rubbed Taylor's elbow.

"You good, babe?"

"I'm good. I'm just going to the restroom," Taylor assured, attempting to calm her anger.

"Excuse me, everyone," she said in a softer voice, before walking away from the table.

Taylor was fuming as she entered the ladies' room. She couldn't understand why her sister could never respect her choices. She was no longer a child, but Nicole had no problem talking to her or treating her as such. She leaned over the sink and stared into the mirror. Taylor took a few deep breaths before running her fingers through her wild, natural curls. Hell, Nicole even hated her choice in hairstyles. She closed her eyes for a couple of seconds, then opened them with the realization that she couldn't please everyone. And Taylor had no desire to try.

"The governor's girl, huh?" a woman said from behind.

Taylor looked up in the mirror to find a tall, pretty, black woman with notable curves standing behind her.

"Excuse me?"

"Yeah. That's you," the woman said smiling. "The governor's girl. I've seen you in the paper. The camera doesn't do you justice."

"Thanks. And you are?"

"My name is Kara, Kara Edwards. I was you before you came along...but better."

Wow, Taylor thought.

The woman added. "Yep, I was his pretty black fetish."

CREED
by *Phoenix Daniels*

Okay. I see where this is going, Taylor thought to herself, while saying "That sucks for you, Miss Edwards."

"He'll never marry you. He's not the marrying kind," Kara assured.

"But... He *has* been married before," Taylor pointed out.

"Yeah, to a white woman. He's gonna use you up. Then he's gonna dump you."

"Is that what he did to you, Miss Edwards?" Taylor asked, seemingly reading the bitter woman's mind.

Kara dramatically rolled her eyes and hissed, "He is so out of your league."

"That may be true," Nicole intervened. "But that four karat, princess cut, flawless diamond on her finger tells me a different story. Did he give you one, Miss... Taylor, what's this hoe's name again?"

"Kara Edwards," Taylor responded, smiling at her elegantly dressed big sister as she spewed ghetto slurs at the "bougie" ass woman. "Miss Edwards," Nicole continued. "Go away, unless you feel like getting a little exercise."

Kara took a second or two to figure out that the exercise that Nicole was speaking of would come in the form of a very good ass whooping. Once hit with understanding, Kara flinched and made her way out of the ladies' room. Taylor looked up at her sister with admiration. It was the same admiration that Taylor had when Nicole used to defend her as a child.

"Nic, I didn't think you still had that in you," Taylor amused.

CREED
by *Phoenix Daniels*

"Shi-id, you can take the diva out of the hood, but you can't take the hood out of the diva," Nicole chuckled.

Nicole closed the distance between them and placed her hand on Taylor's shoulder. She looked Taylor directly in the eye as she spoke. "Tay, I'm sorry about my reaction to the news of your engagement. I gotta stop treating you like my baby sister. You're an adult. Not to mention, an adult that's made far better decisions than I have over the years."

Nicole allowed a tear to crawl down her cheek. Instead of swiping it away, Nicole pulled Taylor in her arms. "I love you so much. And I am happy for you. Victor is an incredible man, and he loves you. So, I love him."

"Thanks, Nic," Taylor sobbed, unable to stop her own tears. "I love you too… so much."

Despite the fact that their family was waiting for them, the sisters held each other longer. And they didn't stop until they got good and damn ready. Taylor had just gotten a loving reminder of how much she and her sister truly loved each other. And although Taylor had friends that were very close, no one would be closer than her big sister.

CREED
by *Phoenix Daniels*

EPILOGUE

"Dinner was amazing, sweetheart," Taylor complimented. "I love it when you cook."

"Oh yeah? You think your family liked my cooking?" Victor asked, peeking out of the kitchen.

"They loved it, babe."

Taylor walked around her living room, picking up empty beer bottles and tossing them into a trash bag. They were cleaning up after she and Victor's informal engagement party.

When she purchased her house, she never would have believed that the very first event that she'd be hosting in her home would be her engagement party. Their official engagement party was to be held at the Governor's Mansion, where they met. Taylor would be lying if she said that she was looking forward to celebrating her engagement with a bunch of strangers. However, she *was* marrying the governor, and she would have to acclimate herself to his lifestyle.

"Taylor, we really could've hired a cleaning service to do this!" Victor shouted from the kitchen.

"Um-mm, I don't like people touching my stuff."

Victor entered the living room, tossing a dish towel over his shoulder.

"That's funny, you never seem to mind when I touch your *stuff*," he teased.

"That's 'cause you know how to handle my *stuff*."

Victor chuckled and hugged her from behind.

CREED

by *Phoenix Daniels*

"It's wonderful how well our families got along," he remarked.

"Yeah, and, oh my God... Did you see the sexual tension going on with Luc and Bella?"

"Not to mention Linc and Kenyatta," Victor grumbled.

"Lord, have mercy," Taylor sighed. "Oh, and our mothers... together, they're gonna be trouble. They were practically planning our wedding without us. And your dad..." Taylor giggled. "He thinks that because of me, you got the Black vote on lock."

"Yeah, but he might be right about that. The old man knows his politics," Victor muttered.

"You wish," Taylor laughed. "Shit, I'm a cop. You might lose a few black votes."

"As long as I have you, sweetness, it doesn't matter."

"Aww, ba-by," Taylor purred.

Taylor sighed and closed her eyes, relaxing against his solid body.

"Gimme this bag. Come here," Victor said, taking the garbage bag and leading Taylor to the sofa.

"Sit. You've been running around all day, making sure that this party turned out okay. You must be exhausted."

"Naw, baby, I'm good," Taylor assured.

"Sit."

Taylor sat and looked up at him with wide eyes. "Should I bark and roll over next?"

"Later," he quipped, tossing a bottle into the bag.

Victor was right. Taylor had had a busy day. Hell, she'd had a busy year. It had been two months since Victor asked her to marry him. She was just barely coming to terms with

CREED
by *Phoenix Daniels*

everything that happened the months before, and now she was about to jump right into wedding planning mode. It wasn't that she was unhappy about her engagement, she just wished that they could have a small ceremony or maybe a destination wedding. She could use a little quiet.

Taylor quietly watched as Victor cleaned. She leaned back against the pillows and thought of all the things that she and Victor had never discussed; one of those things being her job. Victor had never hidden his desire for Taylor to take an inside job, if not quit altogether. She had no intention of quitting, but she did realize that security issues and the press were going to be a hurdle. Since Victor put the beautiful diamond on her finger, it seemed as if they purposely avoided such conversations.

"Taylor, are you okay?" Victor asked, snapping her out of thoughts.

His voice was filled with concern as he sat next to her.

"Yeah…Yes. I'm okay."

"What's on your mind? Talk to me."

Taylor sighed and leaned against him. Victor wrapped an arm around her and massaged her shoulder.

"Victor, it's been a crazy year. The shooting, the media, Maria getting shot, me getting shot, Gore, Candace, you shooting Candace; it's a lot to process. Now we're getting married."

"Is it too soon?" Victor asked with a sad look in his eye.

"No. No, baby. It's not too soon, but… okay…Where are we gonna live? And what about my job?"

"Well, where do want to live?'

"Shit, I just bought this house."

CREED
by *Phoenix Daniels*

"Okay, then we'll live here."

Taylor narrowed her eyes and asked, "Really?"

"Yeah. I like your house. We'll have to make some security provisions, but I'm comfortable here."

"Oh, Victor, you are so fucking awesome," Taylor cooed, climbing into his lap.

"You say that now. But when the subject of the police department comes up, I'm sure you'll change your mind."

"Okay, then we won't talk about that today," Taylor chuckled.

"Good idea. Listen, with all the hell that you've been through, I just wanna give you some of the peace and security that Candace took from you. That part of your life is over. Now we concentrate on our future. Candace couldn't take that away."

"See…that's the thing, babe."

"What's the thing?"

"The whole time we were in Candace's house, she never once copped to shooting me. She was shoutin' from the rooftop about how she shot Maria, but she didn't mention me or Collier at all."

"Hmm…" Victor contemplated. "You sure?"

"I'm positive. So, that leaves the question…how was Candace connected to Collier?"

"She wasn't."

Taylor jumped from Victor's lap at the sound of a female voice coming from her hallway. The beautiful, blonde intruder was standing between Taylor and the weapon that was in her bedroom, so Taylor prayed that the woman wasn't armed with the intention of killing them both.

CREED
by *Phoenix Daniels*

"What the fuck are you doing in my house?" Taylor hissed.

"I came to congratulate you on your engagement to my husband," she said in a sugary, but icy tone.

"What?!" Taylor gasped.

She turned to Victor just as he was slowly rising from the sofa. His normally tanned face had turned as white as a sheet, and he seemed to have stopped breathing. Taylor grabbed his arm when he stumbled slightly forward.

"Victor?" Taylor whispered to him, before shouting, "Who are you?!" at the blonde.

"Sh-she's," Victor stuttered. "Her name is Rosemary—Rosemary Creed. She's my wife."

To Be Continued....

Want to be notified when the new, hot Urban Fiction and Interracial Romance books are released? Text the keyword "JWP" to 22828 to receive an email notifying you of new releases, giveaways, announcements, and more!

Jessica Watkins Presents is currently accepting submissions for the following genres: African American Romance, Urban Fiction, Women's Fiction, and BWWM Romance. If you are interested in becoming a best selling author and have a complete manuscript, please send the synopsis and the first three chapters to jwp.submissions@gmail.com.

Made in the USA
Las Vegas, NV
07 February 2021